Dear arlene,
I hope you
enjoy the
Close of this
series.

Shan G.
Dowdell

SECRETS OF A KEPT WOMAN 3
You Can't Help Who You Love

Also by Shani Greene-Dowdell
Breathless: In Love With An Alpha Billionaire
Keepin' It Tight

SECRETS OF A KEPT WOMAN 3

You Can't Help Who You Love

By Shani Greene-Dowdell

Nayberry Publications

Published by Nayberry Publications (2015)
Opelika, Alabama, 36801, USA
Copyright © Shani Greene-Dowdell, 2015
All Rights Reserved

ISBN: 978-0692394038
Designed by Nayberry Publications

Printed in the United States of America

To everyone who was ever given a second chance to get it right.

You Are Worthy!

Secrets of a Kept Woman 3

PROLOGUE

SHAYLA

"Wait a minute!" Antonio said as he angrily tossed the DNA papers to the ground. "This can't be right. I am not that child's father!"

Antonio could do all of the arguing and fussing that he wanted to do, but according to the State of Georgia, Rhonda's child carried his DNA. While he stood in front of me fuming, I stood quiet and emotionless with my arms flaccid to my sides. It was as if I couldn't think, move or act. "Numbers don't lie," I told him, disappointed in both him and the results.

"I am not that child's father," he said, standing beside the mailbox in the spot where I had screamed to the top of my lungs when I opened the letter.

Numb, I walked to the porch in a trance. "Whatever you do Antonio, don't try to make a fool out of me," I warned. "Those numbers say there is a ninety nine point nine percent chance you are the father of Rhonda's child," I added solemnly.

"That isn't my baby! Shayla, you have to believe me," Antonio said, as part of his Hispanic roots permeated into his English as he spoke.

"Save it, Antonio!" I said to the man I loved, the man I married and thought I would cherish for the rest of my life.

"The test must be a false positive or something, honey. I never slept with Rhonda."

"Oh, how I want to believe you. I want to be able to trust you, Antonio."

"Just do it. Trust me, with all your heart. Trust the man you married." He placed a hand on both of my shoulders and turned me to face him. "This woman has been nothing but a thorn in your side. Don't let her win. We have to stick together until we get this figured out."

I went into the house, completely annoyed by the entire ordeal. Standing in the kitchen looking at the DNA letter, I glared at Antonio. "I don't see how you can deny this."

"It looks like I am guilty of cheating on you, I know this. The evidence is stacked against me, but I need you to believe in me for a minute. When I say..." Antonio walked over to me and turned my face toward him. "...when I say I did not have sex with Rhonda, it is the truth. I mean think about it. I didn't even know what city she or Titus were living in, much less how to contact her. Think back nine months ago. Think back night by night. I was here. With you. As long as we have been married, I have never been out of pocket."

Logically, what he said made sense. "But, the DNA test..."

"Is a lie," Antonio finished my sentence.

I wanted to believe him, but the last man I trusted was indeed having an affair with Rhonda.

My buzzing cell phone gave me a much needed out. "I have to answer that," I said, picking my cell phone up and walking away. "Hello."

"Hi, Shayla. This is Mrs. Jackson."

"Oh, hi Mrs. Jackson." I was surprised to get a call, at this moment, from Rhonda's mother. "What up?"

"I know my daughter has put you through a lot this past week. That is why I'm calling. There is more to the story."

"The DNA papers came in the mail today," I told Mrs. Jackson.

"About that, I was at Rhonda's apartment this morning helping her take care of the baby when I overheard her talking to a lady named Chandra from the Forge Sperm Bank."

"Why would Rhonda be talking to someone from a sperm bank?" Shayla asked.

"She asked Chandra if anyone found out about some missing sperm. They were also talking about how to get child support. I pieced together the conversation and figured out that she got Antonio's sperm from Forge."

"Thanks for that, Mrs. Jackson," I said ending the call in shock. "Shut the front and back door!"

"What did she say? What are Rhonda and her mother up to now?"

"Have you ever given sperm to a sperm bank named Forge?"

"No...well yeah, but that was back in my younger days when I needed cash for school. What does that have to do with...?" Antonio paused as the reality of what I asked hit him.

"Mrs. Jackson thinks it's possible Rhonda got your sperm from Forge."

We stared at each other for the longest time in shock. "How could that happen?" Antonio asked.

"She knew someone who worked there. They must have given it to her," I said looking at him regretfully.

"This is un-freaking-believable baby. How did she know I had sperm there? Why would she do something so crazy?" Antonio asked, as his mind took in all the possibilities.

"I do not know," I said as I looked at Antonio with regret. "I'm so sorry for doubting you when I should have been on your side."

"I would be upset with you, but I am not sure I would have reacted any differently if DNA showed Tyler to be another man's son. The worst part of this is that I have to live knowing she has a part of me in her child and that she plans to use that against you."

I felt so betrayed. "I wanted things to be different with Rhonda this time. I prayed she had changed."

CHAPTER ONE

RHONDA

"Dang mama!" I screamed as I marched up the hall in my dingy two-bedroom mobile home. My mother couldn't hold water, even if she needed it for hydration. She'd just as soon shrivel up and dry out like the old prune she was!

There was a squad car in my driveway and I was sure it was because my mother had told Shayla about me getting Antonio's sperm from the sperm bank. Panic rushed over me as I thought about the possible reasons the officer could be knocking on my front door.

The three dreaded knocks left me wondering if I had spent my last day as a free woman, or if he just had questions.

"Hello ma'am. I'm looking for a Mrs. Rhonda LaShae Wilson. Is that you?" the tall, lanky officer asked once I opened the door. He wore a shit-eating grin on his face as he looked me in the eye.

"Yeah, that's me," I said with a slight tremor in my voice. Thankfully, I'd gotten up and got dressed. I didn't want to have an ugly mugshot posted in that scummy newspaper that winds up on every gas station countertop in Atlanta. My hair was pulled up into a neat bun and I had a nice, light coat of makeup on my face. "Can I help you?" I asked.

"I've got some papers for you from the Justice Department. With your acceptance of these documents, consider yourself lawfully summoned to attend court," the officer said as he placed the papers in my hand. "You will also receive more info in the mail. I was asked to personally deliver these to you," he added with a hump of his shoulders.

"Summoned," I said, as more of a rhetorical question, since I read the words summons at the top of the letter.

"All of the information you need is inside the documents," the officer said as he walked back down the steps toward his car. "Have a good day, Miss!"

I closed the door and leaned my back against it. What was the Justice Department going to do next? I had already been picked up and taken to the police station for official charges to be pressed against me for conspiracy to commit aggravated assault against Shayla. I stayed in that pissy jail for a whole week before I was able to get arraignment and post bail.

I had made a complete mess of everything. James was dead and I was facing more jail time. I was at my wits end trying to hold my life together. I quickly glanced down the hall where Antonia was sleeping, as I began to open the letter. I was so focused on my trembling hands that I didn't notice Titus had walked into the room.

"Who was that at the door, Ronnie?" Titus asked. "I thought I saw a police car outside. Did it have anything to do with Dejah's case?"

"It was a police car out there, but it had nothing to do with Dejah's case. I'm supposed to hear something back from the social worker today," I said, hoping he would walk away without noticing the summons in my hand.

"So you talked to her social worker? What did she say?"

"She said that they are still reviewing her case. They will let us know when they have updates," I lied.

When he continued to stare at me, I said, "Don't worry about it."

I started to walk down the hall toward my bedroom. It had gotten past the point where Titus and I couldn't stand each other. We could barely stand to be in the same room with one another.

All he wanted to talk about was Dejah. Dejah this and Dejah that. Well, Dejah was okay. Probably doing better than both of us, living in a nice foster home.

"How could you say that? How could you say not worry about our child, Rhonda? Foster care ain't nowhere for a child to be," he said, looking at me with so much contempt. He took a deep breath and pushed his dreads out of his face. "You never loved our child!"

"It's not that I don't love her…" I started to say, but paused. *I just don't love you or any part of you*, was what I wanted to say.

I'd fallen out of love with Titus the minute he decided to live a mediocre life. It showed me that I was not good enough for him to go hard. He went hard for Shayla and gave her the finest things in life but, when it came to me, this run-down trailer was all I got.

He wanted me to show so much love to Dejah, who he continually reminded me was the only reason we were together. I had hoped that since she was gone, he would just leave.

"What is it then, Rhonda?" he asked, breaking me away from my thoughts.

"Titus, just give me some time to get things together and some space to breathe. Leave me alone!" I yelled, wishing he would disappear.

"You dizzy ass broad; all you have is time and space," he said, disappointed. "At the rate you're going, you're going to get plenty of time in a little bitty space," he said, walking to the mirror, where he began to tidy up his dreads.

"Whatever," I said as I stared down at the letter. I sat down on the bed, knowing the contents of this letter would dictate my future. "Alright. Here goes," I whispered, as I began to rip open the envelope. Just when I pulled the letter out the envelope and began to read the contents, Titus towered over me looking suspicious.

"Ronda, did the police come here because of James and that shit you in with Shayla's husband?"

"Yes Titus! Now, will you please give me time to read the fucking letter?" I said, jumping to my feet to stand face to face with him. He threw his hands up in the air and walked out of the room shaking his head. I unfolded the papers and began to read.

SUMMONS IN A CIVIL ACTION
To: Rhonda LaShae Wilson
A lawsuit has been filed against you for wrongful birth and conspiracy to commit aggravated assault. Within 21 days after service of this summons on you (not counting the day you received it), you must serve on the plaintiff an answer to the attached complaint. The answer must be served on the plaintiff or plaintiff's attorney, whose name and address are: 2135 Westbrook Drive, Atlanta, Georgia. If you fail to respond, judgment by default will be entered against you for the relief demanded in the complaint. You also must file your answer or motion with the court.
CLERK OF COURT: Loretta Morgan

A bunch of legal mumbo jumbo that I didn't quite understand was included in the summons. Was I being charged in a criminal case, or was I being sued? My anxiety increased after reading the letter, because I didn't understand what it meant. I was scared about how things would play out, disappointed in myself, and annoyed by Titus's reaction. I was a lot of things at that very moment, but I wasn't surprised.

My mother didn't waste any time snitching. Therefore, Antonio had moved forward with suing me and the sperm bank for "wrongful birth."

I looked over at my precious little girl sleeping in her crib. I knew she was conceived the wrong way, but she was not a wrongful birth. She was right, despite all the wrong.

I continued reading the papers. The next document stated that I was not only being sued, but Antonio had filed a restraining order that prohibited me from contacting him or Shayla under any circumstance. I was not to go within a hundred and fifty feet of either of them.

"Well, I'm assuming it is about your baby," Titus said snapping me out of my thoughts. His muscles were bulging out of his white beater and his handsome face was turned up in a smirk. He was still sexy, after all these years. I had to give him that much. I just couldn't stand his annoyingly broke ass. No amount of sexy could compensate for him being broke.

"Huh?" I asked buying myself a few moments before engaging in another inevitable argument. Understandably, Titus had been livid when he found out I had a child by Shayla's husband. Between his going to work for twelve dollars an hour and running around with random hood rats after work, I didn't see why he was so upset about that.

"Don't huh me, woman. You straight up foul for doing what you did, Rhonda. I knew you could be a cold piece of work, by the way you treated Shayla when I was married to her, but this is some maniacal stuff straight out of a psycho movie. After all that has happened, the only reason I'm still here because I care about our daughter. I want her out of the system and you need to be doing your part to make that happen!"

"I'm trying!"

"No you ain't. You too busy caught up in your imaginary new side ho position. You could care less what happens to Dejah," Titus said; spit flung from his mouth with every other word. "Fuck it! I'm going to go get another place and go fight for Dejah myself."

"Yet, here you stand," I said as I folded the letter and stuffed it in my pocket. I rolled my neck as I continued. "Hell, you might as well go. It's not like you're doing anything for me or Dejah. I'd just as soon be alone, with all the help that you're providing."

"That's a lie. I take care of my family."

I paused for a minute and looked him up and down. I didn't have time to fuss with Titus. I had so many other things I had to deal with, but I had to put him in check. "Where were you when I had to write a bad check just to get Dejah's clothes for the winter? It's not like you have any money to buy her anything. Hell, DHR would have taken her then if she didn't come to school with a coat," I reminded him.

Titus glared at me, before pulling out a wad of money. "I do have money. I'm just not giving it to your trifling ass. My child, on the other hand, hasn't wanted for anything, so don't act like you're out here doing the crazy things you do for her. I will dig ditches before that happens."

"Yeah, right. Dig ditches and meanwhile we're living in this dump," I said, making reference to the rundown two bedroom mobile home that we lived in. It was physically intact, but half the appliances didn't half work and if a good wind came through, it was game over. If it didn't flip over, we were going to freeze our butts off. "Thanks for all you do, but no thanks!"

He waved me off. "Rhonda, you have your priorities in life all jacked up. I should have never…"

"Never what? Had sex with me every chance you got? Got me pregnant? Left your precious little Shayla? Married me? Which one?" I asked, knowing that bringing up Shayla would get under his skin. There was one thing he regretted and that was losing Shayla. "Don't you just hate that Shayla is doing very well for herself without you? Got herself a rich businessman and gave him a son. Let's not forget that she's now *Dr.* Shayla Davis."

"I don't hate that Shayla is doing well. I'm happy for her. She deserves it after all she put up with me. See, I don't hate her, but you damn right I miss her. She never would have left our child alone, like you did. She has too much class to go behind woman's back to steal her husband's fucking sperm," Titus tilted his face to the side as his facial muscles contorted into a disgusted expression. "You on the other hand, the hate you have for her is killing you softly. You're nothing but a walking corpse."

"Titus! I am tired of arguing with you about this. If you don't want to be here, leave!"

Titus paused for a minute. "Fine," he said as he walked down the hall with his shoulders slumped in defeat. "Forget this shit."

"Forget this shit," I mimicked, rolling my eyes in disgust at the man he'd become. He gave up on that argument, just like he gave up on everything. He had become so weak. The last thing I wanted to do was to sit around and listen to him bitch about how stupid I was for the next two hours. I had to think about my future, my freedom, which was not looking too good at the moment.

Everything was moving so fast.

I went to the dresser and picked up the phone book, hoping to find a good lawyer that I could afford. I didn't have much money saved. I thought chances were bleak that I would get even a C-list lawyer, until a firm with a familiar name stood out in the directory. Jameson Brown and Associates.

"Jam-e-son," I said, remembering the scrawny kid who used to have a crush on me. He was such a pushover, when we were kids. But now, he was all grown up and doing major things.

Jameson Brown and Associates was a standout firm in Atlanta. Their commercials were frequently on TV with their mascot singing the slogan, *"If you fall, make one call."*

"How could I forget about Jameson?" I asked myself, as I bubbled over with hope. There was a good chance that with a little persuasion Jameson might take my case pro bono; at least, that's what I hoped. I was sure I could do the necessary favors in turn for good representation.

I immediately dialed his office number.

"Jameson Brown and Associates," a cheerful woman said when she answered the phone.

"Ah, yes ma'am, can I speak to Jameson Brown?"

"He's in court today. May I take a message?"

23

"Yes, please tell him Rhonda Wilson called and ask him to call me as soon as possible. He will remember me as Rhonda Jackson."

"Okay, I will give him the message," the woman said.

"Thank you. May I ask when he will be back in the office?"

"He may be back later this afternoon around four, if he doesn't take the rest of the afternoon off. Either way, I will make sure he gets your message."

"You do that," I said as I hung up the phone feeling a little ray of light shining over my gloomy situation. At least I would have a good lawyer, when Jameson accepted my case. There were no ifs or maybes. I knew I was capable of having Jameson groveling to come to my defense.

Antonia's cooing begged my attention away from thoughts of Jameson. I walked over to her bassinette to find her wiggling and kicking in her crib. She was my little bundle of joy; my brightest ray of hope. I'd always wanted a mixed baby and I thought my little half Hispanic, half black creation was perfect as I smiled at her.

I rethought my entire life, as I stood and adored my beautiful baby. Something about Antonia made me want to give her the world. I knew in order to do that I had to beat this case.

Then, I would work on getting my life together and getting Dejah back. I leaned over to pick Antonia up, when Titus walked back into the room to grab his keys off the dresser.

"I packed most of Dejah's clothes. I'll be back for the rest of her things later." He glared at me with venom spewing from his eyes as he ran his hand over his face.

"Rhonda, I think you need psychological help. This time, you need real counseling; no playing around like you did with Shayla."

"Just leave, Titus."

"Is that what you want? You want me to leave you here with your bastard child, so you can forget about Dejah and pretend that you have love." He looked at me with pity. "You can't find love in the middle of hatefulness, and what you did was pure hateful."

"Oh no!" I said rocking Antonia briskly in my arms. "There is no way you are going make me feel bad about my baby. Just because there's no proof of your affairs, it doesn't mean you don't have women on the side."

"What I do, or have done, with other women is neither here nor there now. You have proof in your arms that you were unfaithful to our marriage, but since you're trying to keep score, let's add yours up. Let's see, you've been my wife's best friend, my mistress, my wife, and now my ex-wife husband's baby mama – and you want to label me a cheater? Get outta here."

"We needed the money. That's why I got pregnant with Antonia," I said grasping tightly to my logic.

"Money? You ain't getting no money for this dumb shit!" Titus said, grabbing my arm.

"Stop it, you're gonna make me drop the baby!"

He let go of my arm and blew out a deep breath.

"You know you're not getting any money for this. What is wrong with you?"

"Ever since you copped that plea bargain, you've barely made enough money to get my hair done. I need a man who will take care of me and my children."

"But, you could have found any other man besides Shayla's husband to get pregnant by. Is she the only woman in America whose husbands you want?"

"You should stop worrying about what I'm doing and start working on a real plan for some money. Construction in the day and selling candy and cigarettes out of this house at night is not the move. What kind of man does that?"

"The kind of man that's trying his best to stay legit and take care of his family. You want to see me go back to jail?" He took a deep breath as realization set in his eyes. "Oh, you do, don't you? Or, maybe it's that you don't care one way or the other."

"No, I want to see you back on top," I said, placing Antonia back down into her crib. "I'd give anything for you to be the man again." I grabbed his hand and hoped he'd understand what I was trying to tell him.

"I should take out a notebook and get the blueprint on how to get on top from you, huh?" He laughed heartily. "Well, all I have to offer is the man you're looking at today. It's obvious that we have grown very far apart."

"Yes, we have," I admitted, as my eyes began to water. I let his hand go.

He looked at the subpoena on my dresser. "Expect to get another set of papers in the mail soon. They'll be our divorce papers."

"If that's what you want, Titus," I said waving my hand at him. I wished that he would just leave and stop prolonging the inevitable. I was sure he had a woman somewhere waiting for him.

Hiding the way I really felt, I tickled my daughter's cheeks and said, "Mama loves you, Antonia Bonia. Uncle

Titus didn't have any money, so mommy did what she had to do."

I figured I would annoy him enough to make him leave me alone with my sorrows.

"At least you could have done it the old fashioned way and just had sex. Instead, you stealing sperm like some chick that just got released from the quote unquote nut house," he said before walking out the door.

I heard the front door slam behind him. While I was glad his rant was over, I couldn't help but let the tears fall freely.

CHAPTER TWO

RHONDA

Spending the last five years with Titus after Shayla left him, enrolled in school and went on to become a doctor and marry a successful businessman had not been easy. Sometimes, Titus would look at me with a distant look in his face. I was sure he was thinking about Shayla in those moments, wishing he had stayed faithful. I burned with envy when he'd slip up and call me her name. She left him behind, but her name still permeated his thoughts. I used to wonder what it felt like to have a man love me that deeply. Things like that never happened to me.

Shayla had Titus at the height of his hustling days, when he could afford to pull up in a new Bentley and drop a couple thousand dollars in the mall like it was nothing. I was stuck with him while, as a part of his plea bargain for the murders and drug charges, he would be on probation for the next twenty five years of his life. By the time Titus came to me, he couldn't afford a pack of bubblegum and a soda at the same time, and Shayla actually thought I owed her something.

Titus always reminded me that I wasn't anything like Shayla. He was right. I did sometimes wonder why I couldn't just do right like Shayla. Then, the reasons why I wanted to be nothing like her rushed back to me. The day my love-hate relationship began with her was the day that her actions caused envy to creep into my heart.

I came into Shayla's bedroom one evening when I was sixteen. I had cried the entire walk to Shayla's house, so my eyes were beet red when I walked into the room. I had been living in with her for two months and went to

28

visit my mother, hoping she would let me come back home.

I knew I wasn't going to have much luck when Mr. Travis stood in the kitchen the entire time listening to us talk. Mama had dark circles around her eyes. She looked tired and worn out. She wouldn't even look at me when she weakly said, "You can't come back here, Rhonda." She held her hands in a prayer position allowing her fingers to move back and forth between the grooves in her hand. "I wish our situation was different, but it's not."

"Mama, please, I'm your daughter...your flesh and blood. Look at me!" I said as I stood up from the table. I picked up my book bag flung it over my shoulders when I realized that she was not going to look at me. I never despised a person as much as I despised Mr. Travis when I walked past him. I knew that as long as he was around there was no getting through to Mama. If I had a gun, I would have killed him where he stood.

"Make this your last time coming over here begging yo' mama. We don't want you here," Mr. Travis said as his cryptic looking eyes fluttered, looking me up and down. Mr. Travis was ugly on the inside and out. I didn't know what my mother saw in him. In that moment, I guessed she didn't see much in me either. I finally caught my mother's gaze and she quickly looked away.

Later that evening, after I'd cried the entire walk home, I walked in Shayla's room with so much pain in my heart. Mama Janice, Shayla's mother, was sitting on Shayla's bed helping her with her homework. There was so much love radiating from Mama Janice whenever she was near Shayla.

After a few minutes of helping Shayla, she gave her a big sloppy kiss on her cheek and wrestled her to the bed for a hug. "I love you, Shay," Mama Janice said as she got up to walk out of the room. Then, she looked over and saw me and added, "Love you too, Rhonda."

I was only able to say, "Thanks." The word love had been pushed so far back into my heart I didn't know if it would ever come up again.

Shayla sounded exasperated when she said, "Love you, Mom."

I walked on further into the room and found my sunglasses on the dresser. I quickly changed into my pajamas and laid in the bed, covering my face, while Shayla went on about how much her mother got on her nerves.

"I wish she would just give me some space. She's so overbearing that it makes me sick! Sometimes, I wish she would just leave me alone," Shayla complained.

"At least, she's here for you," I said with my back facing Shayla as I lay in the bed.

"I know but..."

Shayla went on about her mother, until I fell asleep wallowing in my own, real pain. She didn't appreciate the sun, moon and stars that she had at her disposal, while I had dark clouds and rain. Her mother was there for her, cared for her, and cheered for her. Did everything *for her*. Mama Janice was a constant anchor in Shayla's corner, and she did what she could for me too. Shayla's father was always there when she needed him. She had the perfect house. The perfect clothes. She had infinite love and yet she complained.

From that day forward, I saw no problem taking the blessings that she overlooked. I slept with her boyfriends, often causing a rift in her relationships. I kissed up to her mother and father, picking up in areas where Shayla had brushed them off. I set out to show her how it felt to truly be alone. My antics actually caused me to get great attention from men and Mama Janice thought of me like one of her daughters.

Despite of everything I took from Shayla, the day I married Titus and looked into his handsome face, I saw the distance in his eyes. He was with me physically, but his heart was hundreds of miles away. It was with her. He loved her, still. He loved her, even as I stood there rocking Antonia in my arms this morning. He never stopped.

I was sure Shayla was devastated when she found out that not only did I have a child by her first husband, but her second husband had a child that was growing inside of me. She had proven to be resilient over the years, but this time I wasn't so sure she could bounce back. My child would forever be her millionaire husband's daughter. Her son's sister. There was nothing she could do about it.

According to AJC, Antonio Davis had expanded his pool service business throughout most of metro Atlanta, Lithonia, and Decatur and was one of Atlanta's up and coming millionaires.

"We will get what we have coming to us," I told my daughter who was resting peacefully in my arms. Looking into her eyes and seeing Antonio's features so beautifully sculpted across her face was reassurance. Surely, he wouldn't deny his only daughter once he took a look at her precious face.

CHAPTER THREE

SHAYLA

Dear Sweet Heavenly Father,
Take my hand.
Lead me on.
Let me stand.
I am your child.
Covered in your blood.
Please help me to forgive Rhonda for things she's done
to me and the things she is preparing to do to me in the future.
Please cleanse her heart of the hatred that she carries around.
Lord, show her the beauty of Your light. But Lord, even better
than that, keep Your light in my path, so that I will know the
way and so I will not do anything that is unpleasing to your
sight. Help me remember that I am saved and that vengeance is
yours, so I don't end up on Snapped for administering an old-
fashioned beat down to Rhonda Wilson today…
In Your Holy Name,
I pray.
Amen.

I silently covered myself with the same prayer I'd said every day since Rhonda's latest scheme was revealed. Then, I looked at my handsome husband sitting at his desk in our rented condo. He smiled at me as I stretched my arms wide and yawned.

"What time is it, honey?" I asked, as I exhaled a long, soothing breath.

"Time for you to lay back down and get a few more hours of sleep," he said as he stood up and walked over to the bed. "You've worked hard all week, so now you should rest. Plus, we had a pretty long night last night."

I smiled up at him. He was wearing a pair of boxers and his hairy chest beckoned to be touched. I swung my feet around so that they were touching the floor and sat up. My hand instantly extended to rub the hairs on his chest.

"I know, but I need to get up and get breakfast going. Gotta feed my two favorite guys."

His hand touched mine and he leaned down to place a tender kiss on my lips. He pulled me up to stand with him and kissed me deeply.

"Hmmm, after all these years your lips are still sweet in the morning," he said as he studied me with his dark eyes. I smiled at him lovingly. "I went out and picked up breakfast, so you don't have to cook anything," he said, as the smile of afterglow from the prior night's lovemaking sprawled across his face.

"Aw, that was sweet."

"Yeah so, if you want, we can get back in bed and sleep in the entire morning."

"You, me and Tyler?" I said, reminding him that it wouldn't be long before Tyler would be up and on the prowl.

"Yeah, but we'd have a few hours to make some magic happen before he gets up."

I kissed him again.

"Nah, we have to go to church," I reminded him, once I broke the kiss.

"We can catch the afternoon service," he said, taking a seat on the bed. He pulled me onto his lap and began massaging my legs.

"Thank you, honey," I said, rubbing my eyes with my hands trying to fully wake up.

I appreciated the extra lengths Antonio went through to keep me happy. We'd been through so much and had so much more to deal with. I thought my marriage was over, when I got the news that Rhonda's newborn baby girl belonged to Antonio.

The perfect peace I found had been filled with so much noise as Rhonda's plan to pretend she was pregnant and dying of cancer in order to get close to me unraveled. Come to find out, she had stolen Antonio's sperm from a sperm bank he used to get money for college and tried to get James to seduce me. The two of them were planning to blackmail us for millions.

It had been a couple months since that incident and we were taking strides to make things right again, but I still felt some type of way about all that transpired.

"You don't have to thank me," Antonio said holding me tight.

"Do you know how happy you make me?" I asked as I leaned in for another kiss.

He studied me for a long time before saying, "I aim to please." He slid his tongue across his lips and he kissed me while turning to guide me down onto the bed.

"That you do. That you do!" We both laughed as I laid underneath him. "But I need to get up," I said, pushing my way from underneath him and getting out of bed.

"So you're not going to sleep in, Shayla?"

"No, I'm going to get on up and go to Sunday school. I really need it."

"Okay, I had some work I wanted to do this morning, but I guess I'll get dressed and go with you."

"Thanks babe," I said as I walked over and gave him a hug. "I'm going to go get Tyler up and ready for breakfast. Come join us."

"I'm right behind you."

Walking to the kitchen, a brief memory of James attacking me and then dying on my living room floor was so vivid. I was glad Antonio put the house up for sale. I didn't even want to pass by that house again. We had moved into this condo, which was where I planned to be until we found a good buyer.

Lingering thoughts about how Rhonda's betrayal took away the ability for me to have my husband's first daughter popped into my mind as I opened the microwave to warm up the food that Antonio had bought.

If it had been left up to Rhonda, I would have been raped, beaten and possibly killed. Rhonda twisted the knife she already had in my back. This time, she went deeper, twisting it hard and hoping to leave me wiggling and shaking on life's pavement. I loved her and she hated me. I wanted her to succeed and she wanted to see me fail, miserably. She did her best to break me, but God's grace had given me the victory.

"What's on your mind?" Antonio asked, as he walked into the kitchen and noticed me standing by the microwave looking faraway. "Are you okay?"

"I'm fine," I assured him as I took a sip of orange juice. I had learned to grow pretty tough skin defending myself from Rhonda's evil over the years, so I really was fine.

"You okay, Ma," Tyler asked, repeating his father as he took a seat at the table. His big brown eyes stared up at me, as his father placed him in his big boy booster seat. He extended a hand toward me and I gave him my hand. He rubbed my hand lovingly.

"I'm just fine, sweetie!" I adored my son more and more each day.

We sat down and ate breakfast. When we were done, I cleaned the kitchen while Antonio dressed Tyler for church. Once everything was nice and tidy, I walked into my bedroom to find Antonio sitting on the bed putting on his socks. I didn't know how he was going to take what I was about to say, but I said it anyway.

"Antonio, maybe it is time that you speak to Rhonda about your child."

There, I said it, I thought. I had done a lot of digging deep inside myself, and man did I have to dig deep to come to this conclusion. I wanted Antonio to think about the child's best interest.

"I absolutely will not have anything to do with her or her child!" he said, forcefully pulling his sock up his leg.

"Don't get upset, honey. I am on your side, no matter what you choose. I'm just trying hard to be objective here."

"As a psychiatrist, that's what you do. But as a man, I will never give in to Rhonda's mess."

"It's not the child's fault that her mother is a basket case."

I guessed I was thinking about the fact that the child had a part of my husband encoded in her DNA and being raised by Rhonda couldn't be a good thing for any child.

"It's not my fault that she got pregnant by me either." Antonio looked at me as if he were trying to figure me out. "And nothing you say or do will make me feel differently. I sold a part of me for forty dollars at a time when I needed money. I had no intentions to have a relationship with the children that resulted from it then. I most definitely will not be dealing with a woman who went in there specifically to steal my sperm so they could disrespect my wife. You are the most important person in my life and none of your misguided feelings for Rhonda will make me change how I'm handling this."

"I was just…"

"My first daughter will be by the woman I love. You. Case closed. I don't want to hear anything else about it."

"Fine," I said walking into the bathroom and turning on the shower. It wasn't that I didn't agree with what he was saying. It was just that this situation was so complicated.

Once I was in the shower, I turned on the water as hot as I could make it. Antonio walked in and extended his hand toward my bath towel, offering to wash my back. A peace offering. I handed the towel to him and turned away from him.

"Do you remember the day James came to our house to rape you?"

"Yes, I do," I said, as hurt filled my voice without warning.

"Babe, you could have been killed." He lathered the towel and began washing my back. "I hope in all of your thoughtfulness that you thought about yourself. That you thought about us."

"I didn't forget. I just can't get it through my mind that she really wanted him to kill me. I still don't believe that she wanted that to happen," I told Antonio as I turned to face him.

37

"Whether she wanted you dead or not, she was playing with fire and a man ended up losing his life behind it. Do you know how it makes me feel to know that I killed a man?"

"Antonio."

"I. Killed. A. Man. All because that woman thought it was a good idea to blackmail us!" he said. I heard the agony in his voice as he spoke. The same agony covered his face.

"I'm sorry," I said as I stroked his jawline. I pulled him close and hugged him, not caring that I would get him wet. "I won't bring it up again. I am so sorry."

"Baby, I married *you*. I love *you*. And I could have lost you… the woman I love. You are the only woman who has ever carried a child that I will claim. What she stole didn't mean more than a few bucks to me. You and Tyler mean the world." He held me tightly as he spoke.

I tilted my head to kiss his lips. I felt electricity travel through me when he slipped his tongue into my mouth and began a slow, steady assault of my lips. It wasn't long before we were wrapped in one another passionately.

"Daddy, I found my shoes," Tyler said, interrupting our kiss. He'd come into the bathroom and was tugging on his father's leg.

"Okay buddy," Antonio said, without moving his eyes from mine. "You see, this is all I care about. Our family, and those sweet lips of yours are all I will ever care about."

I smiled as my heart swelled full of Antonio Davis. I could have devoured him where he stood. "I love you too, my wonderful husband," I said before giving him a brief peck on the lips.

Tyler turned away, covering his eyes. "Y'all kissing?"

"Okay guys, let me finish my shower and get dressed," I said, shooing them both from the bathroom.

The issue of Rhonda and her child would be addressed soon enough. For the moment all I could think of was how much I loved my husband. I would stand by his side through thick and thin.

CHAPTER FOUR

SHAYLA

It was Monday morning and I was still high from Reverend Brown's sermon about releasing strongholds from your life. My pastor knew he could do some soul-stirring preaching! He even had Tyler up out of his seat waving and clapping his hands. Antonio was more of an internal person, so he just sat next to me and took in the word as I shouted my praise.

I got up early Monday morning and went to the hospital for morning rounds. I checked on my patients early, so I could attend the appointment with our lawyer at one o'clock. An abundant amount of praise was still in my heart as I mentally prepared for our meeting.

As I was pulling into my driveway at noon, the mailman pulled up. It was the first of the month, so our mail was a bunch of coupons intermixed with household bills. There was also a big yellow envelope addressed to Antonio that did not have a return address.

I went inside and stopped in the kitchen to put the bills and coupons in their usual slot. I walked into our bedroom and handed the yellow envelope to Antonio. "Someone sent you this package, but it doesn't have a return address," I told him.

He eyed the package suspiciously before breaking the seal and opening it. Enclosed was a picture of the cutest little girl wearing a bib that said, "I Love My Dad."

"She can't be serious," Antonio said as he slammed the picture down onto the bed. "I'm so sick of that crazy woman!"

I picked the picture up and stared at it for a long while before tearing it in half.

"She's serious," I said as I walked to the trash and threw the picture away. "I think it's time for me to do a face to face with Rhonda. She thinks I'm still the sweet little girl I was in high school. I don't think she knows that I intend to fight for my family."

"No, no babe. Let me handle it. By the time I'm finished with her, she will wish she never messed with us," Antonio said as he took me by the hand.

"Antonio, she doesn't understand when people are civil with her."

"But that's how we are going to handle her," he said, squeezing my hand and looking into my eyes. I reluctantly agreed, knowing he was right.

*

"May I help you?" Brock Gordon's receptionist asked when Antonio and I arrived to his office precisely at one p.m.

"You sure can. I am here to see Brock Gordon. He's my..." Antonio said stepping up to the front desk. A tall, graying man stepped around the corner to greet us before Antonio could finish his sentence. "My man," Antonio said.

"Is it *the* Antonio Davis?" Brock asked with a huge smile on his face.

"Hey, Brock, how are you doing, man?"

"Doing good man." His eyes squinted at me and then widened. "This must be your lovely wife?"

"Yeah man, this is my lovely wife," Antonio said, with a light squeeze to my hand. He took a second to look his friend over. "What are you doing with a head full of gray hair, man we're only thirty one"

"Well, let's see, I just made partner. I have four little ones at home and a wife who demands some fairly exquisite things in life. Does any of that answer your question?" The three of us shared a laugh.

"Yeah, it answers a lot."

"But life couldn't be any better," he added, turning his attention to me. "How do you put up with this guy?"

"He makes it easy," I answered and extended my hand for a shake. "Very nice to meet you."

"Likewise," Brock said. "Come on into my office."

"So you finally got your name on the sign, huh?" Antonio said as we followed Brock through an office door that was close to the receptionist desk. It led into a nicely designed office that matched his stature as partner. "You said you were going to do it and you did. I'm proud of you, man," Antonio added.

"Yep. I did it man, but that's how we Alphas do. We represent the black and gold with a mixture of hustle and dignity. We don't strive for the best, we are the best!" Brock said, making reference to their fraternity.

"Yes, indeed!" Antonio said before they both went into a series of chants and steps representing their fraternity.

"Man, we still got it," Brock said once they were finished. Brock gestured for Antonio and me to take a seat.

"Yep, we do," Antonio said as he sat down.

I eased to my seat in awe of how alive my husband was when he was with Brock reminiscing about his line days. Brock leaned back in his chair, still jovial from their step and chant. "From what I hear, you are not doing shabby either, bruh," Brock said.

"Yeah man, life is lovely. Who would have thought the pool business would be *the* business?" He laughed slightly and then looked at me. "But look, let's get to the matter at hand. Where are we on this lawsuit?" Antonio leaned forward in his chair with a serious look.

"Things are definitely moving in the right direction," Brock said as he shuffled through the files on his desk. "Let me get your file."

"Good, because I got this in the mail today." Antonio handed Brook the picture that he had gotten out the trash and pieced together.

"Is this the baby?"

"Yeah, man. I brought this to you so you can see what type of person we're dealing with. I want you to understand, first hand, why I intend to push hard with this case. I want to own Forge Sperm Bank, at the end of the day."

"Well, you'd be pleased to know that I got an offer from them. I was planning to call you today, until I realized that you were coming in."

"That's good news. What're they talking about?"

"They would like to meet tomorrow to discuss a settlement."

"Does it sound favorable?"

"Yes, very. They want to push this under the table as soon as possible. Can you meet tomorrow at 1 p.m.?" Brock asked.

"I can make time for it, but I want Shayla to be with me every step of the way." He looked at me and asked, "Will you be able to make it, baby?"

"Yeah, that's fine," I said. "I will juggle my work schedule."

"Good. I'm just going to tell you this, Brock. If they are not talking about millions and I mean plenty of them, they might as well get ready to go out of business. Because nothing can change the fact that my wife's biggest hater stole my sperm with the intention of rubbing it in her face, while at the same time conspiring to have her raped and possibly murdered. This is unacceptable."

"I know, Antonio. Why do you think that they are ready to settle? I've applied major pressure to them, that's why. They understand the consequences of not offering a favorable settlement," Brock said confidently.

"I just want to make sure we are on the same page, because when I go in there I will be relentless, man."

"Well you're in good hands, bruh. Let's get it done," Brock said, jotting down a few notes on Antonio's file.

"See you tomorrow at one," Antonio said standing up and taking my hand.

"I hope you know I am going hard on this case for you," Antonio said once we were seated at an eatery down the street from Brock's office. It was lunchtime and I was starving.

"Thanks babe," I said, with mixed feelings.

"I will never forget the look on your face when you thought that I was the father of Rhonda's child. She will pay for making you feel like I betrayed you. She plays with people's lives too much, Shayla."

"Antonio, I appreciate everything you are doing."

I looked at my husband, who had worry lines starting to grow on his face. I realized it was a stressful time for us both. The waitress came and took our food orders and we were soon enjoying a quiet lunch before heading back to our hectic work schedules.

CHAPTER FIVE

RHONDA

"Hello," I said answering the phone quickly when I realized who was calling.

"Hello. This is Jameson Brown. I'm returning a call for Rhonda Wilson," Jameson said in a firm voice. I smiled, wondering if he was still the same scrawny kid that used to wear big bifocals and was always doodling on papers and tucking them under his shoulders as if he were carrying a briefcase. I wagered that he was and that he was hiding behind this strong phone voice. "Hello?" he asked when I didn't say anything.

"Yes, I'm here. This is Rhonda…Rhonda Jackson."

"Oh really?" he said, but I couldn't read the meaning of his short answer.

"Yeah, do you remember me from Tuskegee?" I asked.

"Of course, I do."

"Well, how have you been?"

"I've been good, Rhonda. How about you?"

"Doing pretty good, I guess," I said.

He cleared his throat and was silent for a few moments before he asked, "So, how may I help you?"

"Yeah, well…I need a lawyer to represent me in a case that has been filed against me."

"What type of case is it?" he asked, as his professional voice kicked in and he was one hundred percent business.

"Well, I kinda need to make an appointment to come and talk to you about it face to face," I said, knowing my situation would be difficult to explain over the phone. I did plan to put my clamp in him once I got him alone.

"We can set an appointment," he said, "…but I think it would be more cost effective if you told me about the case now. That way, I can tell you if it is the kind of case I am willing to handle."

Jameson didn't sound like the wimpy kid I knew. The kid that I knew would pick me a fresh bunch of wild flowers and bring them to me when we went out for recess. He asked me to marry him when we were in the sixth grade. I said yes, and then tricked him into believing we were going to have a wedding the following day under the monkey bars. When recess came the next day, he was standing under the monkey bars waiting on me. I gathered a group of our classmates to laugh at him as he stood under the monkey bars seemingly rejected. I was a no-show to our makeshift wedding, and Jameson had been a laughing stock for the rest of the school year.

The confidence and straightforwardness exuding from the other end of the phone, did not sound like the same Jameson I knew. "Well… Are you sure I can't come in and talk to you face to face?" I inquired.

"Rhonda, tell me what's going on."

"I'm accused of stealing something."

"Okay, now we're getting somewhere. Who is the plaintiff?"

"Forge Sperm Bank in Atlanta."

"What are accused of stealing from Forge?"

"I would rather meet with you so I can explain. I think you will understand my side of the story when I explain it in person."

"I usually handle more of the corporate law type cases. I am sure one of my associates will be able to help you though." He paused for a minute as if he were thinking. "I'll tell you what. Come by my office tomorrow at three. You can tell me about your case. I will see if there is some way that I can help you, but I can't guarantee anything."

"Oh, thank you so much Jameson," I said with a deep sigh of relief.

"Don't thank me yet. I'm not sure that we will be able to take your case," he cautioned.

"Okay, three o'clock. See you then," I said, cheerfully. "And Jameson, this means a lot to me."

"Sure. Make sure you bring any paperwork from the court and/or Forge that you've received. I need to review those," he said.

"Okay, see you at three tomorrow."

I hung up the phone and jumped for joy.

CHAPTER SIX

TITUS

On everything in life, it was not easy living with Rhonda. She was a walking basket case. Back in the day, when we were sneaking around, she had what I would call that 'can't leave home without it.' Creeping with her caused me to forget I even had a wife. Between her thighs was my home away from home. I used to lay back and let Rhonda do her freaky shit and then go home and let Shayla pamper me from head to toe.

Everything was going good, until Rhonda got pregnant and Shayla left me. I went into a deep slump after I got my divorce papers. Those papers were a reality check, a swift kick in the butt that revealed everything important in my life was slipping away. I went from being on top to losing in my personal life *and* in the dope game.

Two months after I signed the divorce papers, a judge dropped his gavel giving me two years in prison and twenty five years' probation for the murders of Big Shirley's crew and drug charges. Even with the best lawyer around and putting over a million dollars in his pocket, I was going to be on the ball and chain of a probation officer for twenty five years! Just to get that raggedy deal, I had to snitch on most of my friends. Needless to say, I made enemies with people in very high places.

I didn't care what they called me in the streets, once I found out I was going to be a father, I gave all them niggas up. I couldn't risk having my daughter grow up without me. Knowing that my baby was growing inside of

49

Rhonda's stomach and that I was facing major time, made dropping the dime on Jay and Turp a little easier. It was hard doing that to my folks, but hell, they probably would have done the same thing if they were in my position. However, I had no problem giving up Lil Red's traitorous ass. I would have called him out in a lineup in his face, if given the opportunity. I was no snitch but, to be on this side of the bars with my daughter, I would do it all over again.

I served a year and got out with good behavior. I crossed over to a very low-key lifestyle and moved to Atlanta, Georgia once I served my time. I started working at Freeman Construction, drove a 2005 Honda, and wore regular clothes. My dreads were long like Bob Marley's, hanging naturally from my head. I had no aspirations of being flashy, ever again. I was too busy, making sure I had the proper permission to do everything I had to do, to be flashy.

I had go get permission to move from one side of the city to the other, permission to take a trip, and permission to blow my damn nose! In order to keep my freedom, I had to walk a straight line, which was something I was not used to.

I remained true to Rhonda, through it all. I knew a woman that rode with her man while he was facing prison time should be made official. Therefore, a few months after I signed my divorce papers, I married Rhonda. Things were okay for a while, but after I got out of jail and started spending time with Rhonda, I knew I'd made the biggest mistake of my life. I had let a grade A woman go for an insanely insecure, detached and conniving trick. Shayla was practically a saint compared to Rhonda.

This latest stunt Rhonda pulled leaving our daughter at home, so she could go steal sperm and then come back with another man's child was some next level bull. There I was thinking someone had kidnapped my wife and that she was somewhere lying in a ditch stankin'. I called everyone trying to find Rhonda, feeling that she wouldn't knowingly leave our daughter home alone. I filed a missing person's report at the police station and got a private investigator involved after she was gone a few days. I wanted my daughter's mother returned home safely, by all means.

The thought that Rhonda could have been killed devastated me, so when I found out she was perfectly fine and staying in a nice hotel in Atlanta, I moved out of our home for good and moved in with my girl, Monika Ryle.

Monika was a nice, young lady in her mid-twenties that I met one Saturday at the mall. Just on some complete randomness, one Saturday I got up and went to the mall trying to find some peace in the middle of the wild storm that had become my life. From that day forward, when I needed someone to talk to, Monika had been a listening ear. She gave me good advice and even tried to help me find Rhonda when she was missing.

I pulled into to Monika's apartment complex and found a parking space in front close to her door. I got out and went to knock on the door. I was ready for her beautiful smile to brighten my day. She had been the only bright spot in my life, since Dejah had been taken into the system.

She was selfless and had a genuine heart. Not only that, she was ambitious. The girl had a scholarship for a local nursing program and still worked thirty two hours a week. She was smart with her money and had her own place and car. As soon as she opened the door, I smiled and pulled her face to mine for a long, passionate kiss on her savvy little lips.

"What was that for?" she asked once I broke the kiss.

I picked her up off her feet and kissed her again. She wrapped her legs around my back and hugged my neck tight as she returned the love. She her curly hair smelled as sweet as a fresh flower as it fell down on either side of my face.

"Because I needed it," I told her as I allowed her to slide to her feet.

"Well, I missed you too," Monika said with a sly grin. "I don't like it when you are not here."

"I don't like it either, but I had to go over there to see what Rhonda was doing to get my daughter back."

"Did you sleep with her?"

"See, that's the first thing you always ask."

"Did you?"

"No. I slept in my daughter's room, as always. Why would you ask me that?" I said as I thought about how crazy the accusation was. Rhonda was sexy, but there was nothing about her that was sexually appealing to me. She'd zapped all sex appeal out of her voluptuous body when she left my daughter at home to fend for herself. *No real man love a woman who mistreats his child*, I thought.

Monika walked away from me and picked up the remote control. She turned off the television and walk back over to stand in front of me. "You've been gone for two days and I wanted to know."

"I haven't been gone for two days. I was just here yesterday."

"But you didn't stay overnight. At night, you went to her house."

"She is still the mother of my child and, unfortunately, my wife." I knew she hated for me to say the W word around her. She didn't think Rhonda deserved to have Mrs. attached to her name.

"You're right, *she* is your wife. So, who am I?"

"You are my heart. You are the girl I love."

"Am I?"

"You should never question that. You should always be confident about who you are to me."

We'd only been messing around six months, but my feelings for her were strong. I showed and proved that to her every chance I got.

"Titus, you say that like our situation is normal. This is not easy. It's hard knowing my position when you spend nights in that house with her. My mind goes in so many places when I'm lying in bed *alone.*"

"It's not easy for me either," I told her before grabbing her chin and pulling her lips to mine. I kissed her deeply, wrapping my arms around her back. I pulled her as close as possible.

What Monika didn't understand was that I missed my daughter so much that it was killing me. It was hard for me to explain that I went to my house some nights and laid in Dejah's bed just inhale her scent from her pillows. It hurt me not knowing what was happening to her at any moment.

"I love you and I don't want you to ever forget that, Monika," I whispered in her ear.

"I love you too," she said as her hand slipped underneath my shirt touching my back. "I really love you," she said looking into my eyes.

Her pretty, round face glowed under the dim light in the living room. Her soft, plush body caused my mouth to water and my body to stiffen. I stared into her eyes, as I moved her hand to cover the bulge in my pants. I was sure she saw the same fire burning in my eyes as I saw in hers as she touched me. I wanted to rip her little pink shorts and tank top right off her body, when she unzipped my pants and took my shaft into her hand.

My erection was as hard as a steel post. I needed to be inside of her. I pushed my pants down to the floor and stepped out of them, along with my boxers. I slid my hands down the sides of her shorts and eased them to the floor. I kissed her legs on the way down and on my way back up, stopping to place a passionate tongue kiss on her sweet pussy.

"Titus!" she screamed when my tongue pulled slightly at her bulb. "I *do* love you, Titus."

"Muah." I placed one last kiss before making my way up her stomach, lifting her shirt as I stood and pulling it over her head. Her firm breasts spilled out of the shirt. I took each one in my mouth and sucked as if I were feeding on the vivacious life she so freely gave. I didn't have a care in the world, when I was with Monika.

She backed into the sofa and laid down on it, pulling me down on top of her, all while offering her sweet, pretty lips. I settled on top of her and wrapped my arms around her waist, pulling her as close to me as our bodies would mesh. I felt my dick swell to the max. I knew I had to release the pressure building within, so I tossed her legs across my shoulders and plunged into her heat without warning.

"Ummh," I moaned upon entering her. She felt so good; my moans became more guttural with each thrust. I bucked in and out of her, satisfied that the next plunge delivered as much euphoria as the last.

"Titus! Ah, Titus," she screamed as she matched my thrusts, while holding tightly onto my back.

Hearing her call my name made me plunge harder and deeper. The harder and deeper I plunged, the closer to euphoria I traveled. I could feel goose bumps pop up all over my body, as she bucked underneath me. Hot cum gushed into her welcoming canal in one long, gratifying release.

Once I came, she jerked and contracted letting me know that her orgasm had arrived on time. I didn't even move once our love was made. I just laid there inside of her, kissing her over and over.

"Monika, I've gotten it wrong many times, but this time I know it's right," I said, laying on top of her with my mouth close to her ear. She didn't reply, she just held me closer to her. We stayed like that for a long time, until I got up to get a blanket.

*

"I gotta get Dejah out of these white folks system," I told Monika as I turned the television looking for a good movie to watch. It pained me to think that some pervert could have his hands on my child, at that very moment.

"What are they saying you need to do in order to get her?"

"I gotta have a stable place for her to go to. I gotta prove I can provide what she needs and that her environment will be safe. With all that Rhonda is going through with the courts, they're not going to let her come back to our house," I said, taking a look around at Monika's house.

"So, pretty much you're gonna have to tell them you have a place for Dejah to go," Monika said.

"What if we both stay here with you?" I said looking at her intently. "I mean, I've been staying here a lot anyway, and we have hit it off pretty good. I could help you out with your bills more. What do you think?"

"I'm okay with that, Titus," Monika said as she snuggled up closer to me. "I'd love to have you here, with yo' fine ass."

"What about Dejah?"

"Anyone that's a part of you, is a part of me," she said.

I smiled and gave her a peck on the lips. I mulled over the idea of staying with Monika. It didn't sound bad, at all. It wasn't like I had any type of relationship with my wife. I hadn't slept with Rhonda in over a year. I had been sleeping in my daughter's room, until I came over to spend a week with Monika last year. That was when Rhonda and I had an argument about some texts I found where she was talking about getting back at Shayla. When I confronted her about it, she got hostile, so I left the house and came to stay with Monika.

The next thing I knew, I was getting a call from a neighbor telling me that Rhonda left Dejah home overnight by herself and the police were called. The bitch had checked out of reality and my child was in the system, in the blink of an eye. I'd been trying to get Dejah back home since then, but with my felony charges and probation and Rhonda's case pending it was a complicated process.

"While I'm over here trying to figure out how to get my child, Rhonda's ass is over there goo-gooing over her new baby. It's like she forgot that she already has a child," I blurted out.

"Some people don't know a good thing when they have it, baby," Monika said. "But, I am here for you. Whatever you need, just let me know. I will help you get Dejah back."

"Thanks babe. We'll go down there tomorrow and let her social worker know she will be coming here."

*

The next morning, I got up and went to the store. I wanted to cook Monika breakfast and take it to her while she was in bed. I went into the kitchen and opened the cabinets. She didn't have any of the foods that I needed to cook. I laughed out loud.

"Dang, she doesn't have anything. I'm going to have to change this," I said as I wrote a list of the things I needed from the store. I learned how to cook a long time ago, because Rhonda was not a cook either.

I drove to the market and picked up some bacon, eggs, grits and orange juice and walked to the register. The redbone that rang my order was looking hella sexy when she said, "Good morning, Sir. Did you find everything alright?"

"Yeah," I said as I placed all of my groceries on the conveyer belt.

She rang everything up as slow as she possibly could. I kept looking at my watch wondering what the hell was the hold up. "Your total is thirty one seventy five," she said. I handed her the money and, when my receipt printed off she took her pen and wrote some numbers on it. "Just in case you didn't find *everything* you want, I put my number on your receipt," she said with a wink.

"Oh, no. I'm good lil' mama," I said, thinking about Monika and how she was willing to invite my daughter into her home. I threw the receipt in the trash as I walked out the store.

Ole girl was bad. Any other time, I would have been storing her digits in my phone and by the end of the week I would have been knocking redbone's box out the park. I figured right then and there that my playing days were officially over. I wanted to be true to Monika.

I smiled as I put my bags in the trunk, jumped in the car and headed back to the Monika's place.

CHAPTER SEVEN

SHAYLA

I was sitting at my desk mulling over documentation for my entire client list, one at a time. I'd been dinged at least twice last week alone by the Medical Records Department at the hospital saying that I hadn't completed this or completed that. If I'd known becoming a doctor would mean I'd spend most of my time writing dissertations about my patients I would have thought twice about it. I wanted to help people not write essays about their life, day in and day out. I felt that was time I could spend counseling a patient one-on-one. Too bad the powers that be didn't see it that way.

As I was flipping through my tenth chart in an hour, my good friend, Lissa, walked in.

"Hey Shayla!"

"What's up?" I asked barely taking my eyes off the electronic chart. Indulging in quality time with Antonio had put me two hours behind, so I knew that going to lunch with Lissa was not an option.

"Don't you what's up me. What's up with you? You are the one who hasn't returned any of my phone calls."

"I've been a super busy, you know. As this year of residency flies by, my workload has doubled. In between work and this mess with Rhonda, I've been finding it harder and harder to keep everything caught up."

"Is there anything I can do to help?" Lissa asked as she plopped down in the chair in front of my desk.

"I wish you could. Unfortunately, I must pay the cost to be the boss." I smiled, happy that very soon the word resident would be dropping off my MD status.

"Well, I could run errands for you or something," Lissa offered.

I placed my pen to my cheek as I considered her offer. I did have a shitload of errands and cleaning that could use a helping hand. "Nah, Jessica will get to them," I told her. "I have increased the hours that she has been at the house lately. I don't know what I would do without her."

"Fine. Now that we have that settled, guess who has a new man?"

"Oh, God," I said as I buried my face into my laptop. "Not a new man."

"You act like you don't want me to be happy."

"Darling, I want you to be happy more than you know. I just want you to find a good man."

"Well, this is a good one, if I do say so myself. And he is well able to provide for me and my children whenever I decide to have children."

"But is he married?"

"What do you think chick?"

"I don't know. That's why I asked."

"No, he is not married," Lissa said as she stood straight up and crossed her arms. "And if you are going to shoot me down like that, I'll just catch you later."

Softening my tone, I said, "I'm not trying to be rude. I was just checking."

"For your information, I've already checked. I checked the city records. I've checked his ring finger. I've checked his house for any sign of a woman. I even looked in his glove compartment to make sure that no woman has left lipstick or fingernail polish in there."

"Sounds like you are serious."

"Kinda, sorta. He wants to take things slow, and so do I," Lissa said, uncrossing her arms.

"Do I know him?"

"He's from Tuskegee and he says he knows you."

"Really? What is his name?"

"Jameson Brown."

"Aw! Jameson's father is my pastor. He was a dorky little kid when we were growing up. Of course, I know him. He used to be crazy about Rhonda when we were in school."

"We have been dating for the past month."

"A whole month? How did you slide that one past me?"

"I met Jameson at a speed dating event that was hosted by Soulful Affairs. You know how lonely I've been since Seth. I may have smiled when I was around you, but I was crying on the inside. I wanted to make sure I took time to get to know the next person. Jameson and I hit it off immediately, but we are not rushing things. In fact, we still haven't… you know."

"Well, I can see that from Jameson, but you…a whole month…priceless. That must be some kind of record for you, Lissa. Kudos!"

"Whatever, smart butt. I learned a lot from Seth."

"Really, what did you learn?" I asked, interested in knowing what my friend took from her last relationship where she jumped in bed on the first night with Seth Baker, fell in love with him, only to find out that he was married.

"I learned that how you start is definitely how you finish. I'm starting out this time getting to know Jameson and not his body." Lissa's eyes fluttered as she talked about Jameson. "And I like what I see so far. He's a very good person."

"Well, I'm happy for you. I would never imagine Jameson treating you the way Seth did. He is a good person, indeed." I looked at my computer and started clicking a few selections for my charting.

"Well, let's just hope that you are right about him treating me right, Shayla."

"I know I am right," I said, continuing to type values into the computer.

"Either he will treat right, or I will pull a Houdini on him and be out so fast he won't even remember I was there."

"I hear you talking and I like what I hear," I said, hoping that she would keep her word, not for me but for herself.

"Are you planning to go out for lunch today?" Lissa asked.

I looked at the mountains of work on my desk. "Nah. It's bad enough that I came in late today. I will just grab something from the machine or something."

"Cool. I'll check in on you later this week. We have to do lunch soon."

"Okay, that sounds awesome."

I watched Lissa as she walked out of my office. It was only a little while ago that she was in love with Seth. She'd been through a lot and I hoped she was not moving too fast with her feelings for Jameson.

CHAPTER EIGHT

RHONDA

"What are you up to now?" my mother asked as I bent over to spray a generous amount of Beyonce Heat between my thighs. I placed the bottle back on my dresser and admired the natural tones of my perfectly applied makeup by Mary Kay.

The makeup application purposely didn't match my choice of provocative clothing, which was a form-fitted, fire engine red midriff dress, with matching red stilettos. I turned to look at my backside and, no doubt, my best asset was my beautiful, plump and panty free derriere. There was no doubt that I was feeling myself.

"Mama, don't worry about what I'm about to do. You just do your grandma thang and make sure that you give Antonia her bottle at two p.m."

"What time are you coming back?" Mama asked desperate for some type of details about where I was headed.

"I should be back soon. This won't take long," I told her. I didn't want to give her too much information that she could report back to Shayla.

"But, you still haven't told me where you're going?" she pressed.

I turned swiftly and looked her dead in the eyes. "To handle some business, damn! Now stop with the questions."

She threw her hands high in the air. "Please just make sure you are not going to do anything stupid. What you need to be doing is calling Shayla to apologize."

I grabbed my purse and headed to the door. If I would have said what I wanted to say, we'd be rolling on the carpet before it was over.

"I have to go," I told her before closing the door behind me.

It was almost time for my meeting with Jameson. The ride to Jameson Brown and Associates was quick. Traffic wasn't as tight as it normally was during the midday in Atlanta and I was glad of it. When I pulled up to the building that his office was located in, I was impressed. I did a double take to make sure I was in the right place.

"Not too shabby at all," I said, taking in the large building that was beautifully sculpted, with perfect landscape.

The fresh smell of money hit me in the face when I entered the front door. There I was, a country girl without a penny to my name, in an office building shared by moguls in many different fields. I looked at the directory on the wall and found that Jameson Brown and Associates was located on the second floor. I stepped on the elevator and rode up with two other women who appeared to work in the building.

"Hi, are you here for Mr. Brown?" one of the women asked with a slight grin on her face.

"Yeah. Why do you ask?" I asked, suddenly feeling as if she was stereotyping me, since I was black and visiting a black lawyer's law office. "Is it because I'm black that you think I'm coming to see a black lawyer and probably the only black lawyer in this fancy ass building?" I asked her with my pointing finger raised and neck rolling.

"No, I just took a wild guess because his office is on the second floor."

"The only office on the second floor," the other woman added with a raised brow.

"Oh," I said giving her a half smile. My wagging finger stopped and fell to my side. I stepped off the elevator and sheepishly said, "Have a good day."

The two ladies looked at each other and shook their heads. It didn't bother me any, because the feeling was mutual. What they didn't know was that if I wasn't getting off when I did, and they looked at me like that and shook their heads, I would have told them something very unpleasant.

"I'm Renee, and you must be Rhonda Wilson," a well-kept, slender woman sitting at the front desk said snapping me out of my thoughts.

"Every day of the week," I said greeting her genuine smile with one of my own.

"Great! Mr. Brown has been awaiting for you. Please fill out this quick assessment and then bring it back to me when you are done and I will take you right back."

I looked down at the paper she handed me and my face tightened. The genuine smile I had when I saw the woman was quickly fading. I didn't have time to be filling out no damn papers.

"Uh, this will not be necessary. Jameson knows who I am," I said as the phony smile slipped from my lips.

"I am sure he does ma'am," the young lady said, but every new client must fill out an assessment. Please fill out the top two pages and I will fill in the rest. Thank you," she said.

I would not have taken the papers, if she hadn't been so nice about it. I found a seat in the reception area and filled out the forms. I returned to the desk after about five minutes.

"I'm done. Renee, right?"

"That's right."

She took the forms and tapped a few notes into her computer. "Mr. Jameson just called me to see if you made it, so let's get you back there now."

"Sure," I said, noting that he had called to check on me.

I knew he could hardly wait to see me. After all, I was his kindergarten through twelfth grade crush. I was sure that it was safe to say I'd been the object of desire in many of his childhood wet dreams. Meanwhile, his puny face and shinning silver braces had been two things I couldn't wait to forget. I looked at the yearbook earlier this morning just to remember how he looked and he was as hideous as I remembered.

Before I knew it, we were standing in front of a door with a huge gold plate that read, Jameson Brown, Esq. *Aw, a little man, big sign*, I thought.

There were two men standing in there talking, when Renee opened the door. I forced a fake smile at the short man with the huge pair of glasses on his face. He smiled back at me and it was just like old times. He was attracted. I was disgusted. I opened my mouth to speak but was interrupted by Renee.

"Mr. Jameson, here are the reports you asked for," Renee said, handing them to the taller gentleman. "And, I brought Mrs. Wilson back for you, as well."

"Thanks so much. Please have a seat. I will be with you in just a second," the cinnamon colored, handsome man said.

I looked at the short man who was giggling all over himself at my reaction. "I'll get on these right away, Mr. Brown," he said taking the reports out of Jameson's big hands.

"So you're Jameson?" I said in shock once we were alone.

"Every day of the week," he said, mimicking what I'd told his receptionist earlier. She had told him what I said, I thought. I stood there in shock for at least thirty seconds. It wasn't that I thought my plan couldn't work. It just would not be like taking candy from a baby with this Jameson. The tall, medium-build fine specimen standing in front of me was anything but a pushover. The way he gave orders to his secretary and mentee was proof of that.

"After all of these years, it is really great seeing you Rhonda," he said stepping closer to give me a nice, long hug. The smell of his Burberry cologne shot straight into my system.

"I...well...same here," I said taken way back by his deep, alluring voice, cute dimples that formed on the sides of his lips when he talked, and the wonderful way he stood there looking at me.

"What have you been up to all these years?" he asked, giving my body a once over.

"Just doing me," I said.

"And you're doing it beautifully," he said.

Oh, so he's a flirt, I thought as I looked around his office. "You're not doing too bad yourself," I said.

"I never intended to do bad. What did you think I was writing on all of those sheets of paper that I used to carry under my arms?" He gestured with his hands for me to take a seat.

"Oh, I don't know. I thought it was just scribble scrabble. You were so different back then."

"No. I was making plans to build this firm." He took a deep breath. "So, you wanted to meet face to face, so you could tell me about your case. Explain everything from the beginning and I will tell you what I can do for you."

More things than one I hope, I wanted to say, but I said, "There is no good way to say this. The allegations against me are so crazy."

"Look, I have been in law for a while, so there's probably not much you can say that I haven't heard already. I will precaution you that you must be honest with me and the rest will take care of itself. The one thing I hate more than anything is to get blindsided in the courtroom. Do you understand?"

"Yes, I do," I said as I tried to figure out how to tell him I was being accused of stealing sperm from a sperm bank with the intent to impregnate myself and extort money from man.

"Okay, so go ahead and tell me everything."

I handed him the papers that the police delivered the day before. Jameson dropped his pen onto his note pad as he read the details. "I'm being accused of stealing sperm from Forge Sperm Bank."

"This *is* crazy. What is going on here?" He looked at me with questions in his eyes. "What's your explanation of what happened?"

"Some jerk is accusing me of stealing his sperm from a sperm bank, of all places." I stood up and took a slow spin. "Do I look like I have to steal sperm to get pregnant?"

Jameson didn't look affected by my display of sexuality. Instead, he looked dumbfounded by my admission of the charges against me. "Why do they think the sperm used to produce your child is stolen?" he asked.

"I have no idea. I guess that's the best the father of my child could come up with after cheating on his wife. He told her his sperm was stolen, when in fact we had a sexual relationship."

His accusatory eyes landed on mine. "I see."

"I didn't know he was married," I assured him as I sat down and crossed my legs, making sure that he could see enough bare skin to spark his imagination.

"I see," he said again as he picked up his pen and wrote a few notes on his pad.

"He led me on and told me he loved me."

"But your last name is Wilson. It used to be Jackson. Are you…?"

"Married? Yes, I am, but my husband left me over a year ago for some girl that's on section eight here in Atlanta. I was looking for companionship and that was when I fell for Antonio Davis."

"Antonio Davis. The name sounds familiar."

"It probably does. He is a well-known businessman in Atlanta."

"You mean Antonio Davis, as in the Antonio Davis who owns the largest landscaping and pool service in the metro Atlanta area?"

"Yeah."

"The one with the popular commercial with the slogan, don't be a fool, call us to clean your pool."

"Yeah, that's him."

I perked up when he spoke about Antonio's business. I knew Antonio was financially well off, which was why I needed this case to be in the bag. My daughter could rightfully become one of the heirs to his millions.

"So, you are saying that you had a relationship with him, got pregnant, and now he is saying that his sperm was stolen?"

"That's exactly right. I thought he loved me," I feigned emotional distress as I thought about the many people who abandoned me in my life.

"But, he's married to Shayla. You guys used to be so close. How is she taking all of this?"

"We haven't been friends for a while, so I don't know how she's taking it. When I started a relationship with Antonio, I didn't know he had a wife. Besides, this is not about Shayla."

"I just brought her up because it was her husband that you had an affair with, but okay," Jameson said with a raised eyebrow. He adjusted his tie and I knew he was uncomfortable taking my case.

I stood up and walked around to his side of the desk and sat on it. My legs were inches away from his face. "I can sense that you don't feel comfortable about my case. You knew me and Shayla in Tuskegee, I get it. But, I can think of a few reasons why taking this case might be beneficial for the both of us." I opened my legs a little wider exposing my bare flesh.

"Well, tell me something," he said, not taking his eyes off my legs. "Will you be real with me and tell me what I'm up against, if I decide to take your case?" he asked, finally looking into my eyes.

I spent the next fifteen minutes sitting on Jameson's desk telling him my side of the story. I told him that I was a woman searching for love who fell for a man that took advantage of me. I told him that Shayla and I had not spoken since she broke up with Titus and that when I ran into Antonio I had no idea that he was her husband.

"I would never have an affair with her second husband after what I went through with Titus," I told him. That was my story and I was sticking to it.

I looked at Jameson as he sat there in his preppy jacket, collar shirt and tie. I slid down from his desk and walked to stand behind him. I massaged his shoulders, slowly and meticulously, before spinning his chair around to face me.

When he didn't put up a protest, I said, "I really like the man that you have grown to be." I lifted one of my stiletto heels and placed it on his thigh. "And I promise that if you take my case pro bono, I will make sure that you enjoy every moment of it."

He glanced over my body with quick judgment. It was as if his mind was warring between the rising sexual tension in his loins and whatever they taught him at the Bar Association. I couldn't read him, so I didn't know where the conversation was about to go. If I had it my way, it would lead to his sweet brown body atop of mine right on his desk.

"You and me, we go way back Rhonda," he said swallowing the lump in his throat. He adjusted his collar and placed a hand on top of my shoe. He gently placed my leg back onto the floor. "I would love to help you, but before I make a decision based on the way you're making me feel right now, I want to ask you something."

"Ask me anything," I said with a fire burning deep in the pit of my erotic soul.

In all seriousness, he looked straight through me and asked, "Will you attend church with me this Sunday?"

"Church?" I asked as the devilment I'd planned for the evening began to slip away to a faraway place. The heat that was building between my thighs felt as if an air conditioner had suddenly been turned on.

"Yeah, church. My father is my spiritual guide. He is the pastor at Real Deliverance First Baptist Church and before I make this decision I would like for us to talk to him."

"Uh, sure," I said as I walked back around to the front of his desk. I was sure the look on my face was awkward as I placed my purse on my shoulder.

"Hold on before you go, Rhonda!" Jameson called after me before I walked out of the door.

"Yes."

"Rhonda, Lord knows you're as beautiful as the Lord would allow on the outside." His eyes raked over my body once again. "But on the inside, you appear to be an empty shell, seeking to be fulfilled by all the wrong things. So, when I invite you to church, it's not just to get my father's opinion on your case. It's because I'm an old friend trying to help find another way to fill your cup. I hope you receive that."

I nodded.

"I hope I haven't offended you."

"You haven't," I said, readjusting my purse strap on my shoulder.

"Great, I'll pick you up," Jameson said. "I'll call you later this week to get directions to your house."

"O...kay," I said as I walked out the door and headed to the elevators feeling as cheap as a half dollar.

CHAPTER NINE

TITUS

"Let me get this straight. What you are saying to me, Mr. Wilson, is that you can show that you have a stable home environment separate from Dejah's mother?" Mrs. Rainey, the skeptical social worker asked when I showed up at her office at eight fifteen demanding an appointment.

"Monika Riles here has agreed to let us move in with her. We are going to share the expenses and Dejah and I will be moving into her two-bedroom apartment," I handed her the agreement that Monika had drawn up.

"Is this right, Ms. Riles?"

"Yes ma'am," Monika said as she looked at me. I squeezed her hand silently showing my appreciation for all that she was doing.

"This all looks favorable, Mr. Wilson. Judge Handy is in court today. I will see if I can get Dejah's case file added to the cases being seen. If so, and everything checks out with you and Monika, then all we'll have to do is do a home visit and Dejah could be coming home tonight."

I could feel my heart about to leap out of my chest. Having my baby girl back with me meant the world. "That's would be great Mrs. Rainey."

"Just between me and you. This is not usually how it works. There can sometimes be a much longer process, but after hearing all that you have said today, seeing how you've been consistently attending the supervised visits, checking on your daughter and trying to get her out of this system I want to help you." The female social worker stood and extended a hand to me. "I'm going to do all that

I can to get her home by the end of the day, but you have to promise that she will have no contact with the mother, until Rhonda's legal battles are sorted through."

"You don't have to worry about that. I promise that will not be a problem," I said, as my anger level rose just thinking about Rhonda.

"Okay, I will see what I can do and give you a call later today."

*

Mrs. Rainey was true to her word. It was about six p.m. that night when Dejah walked through the doors of Monika's apartment with the kind-hearted social worker. She had gotten Dejah's case in front of a judge who agreed that as long as Dejah was staying with me and Monika that Dejah could be released. It also helped that Monika had accepted responsibility for Dejah's wellbeing.

"Daddy!" my little girl yelled as she rushed into my arms.

"Aw, baby. I miss you so much," I said. My daughter was in the care of DHR for far too long. To have her with me, where she belonged, caused an unexpected tear to fall from my eye. "I'll never let anything like this happen again," I told her as I placed a million kisses on her tiny face.

"It's okay daddy," she said patting my back, when I hugged her.

"You are a good woman, Mrs. Rainey. Thank you so much for what you have done for my family."

"Mr. Wilson, you are one of a kind when it comes to fathers fighting for their daughters. We need more like you."

"I appreciate that," I said, still holding Dejah close.

"I love my daddy," Dejah told the social worker. "'Cause he always loves me," she added looking at me and I nearly had a meltdown.

"There are a few papers for you to sign and then I'm going to let you all catch up." Ms. Rainey pulled a folder out of her briefcase and handed it to me. I put Dejah down and walked to the table. She handed me a pen and I signed all of the necessary places that would release my daughter into my custody. The documents said that Rhonda had been contacted and told that she was to only have supervised visits with Dejah, until the court ruled further. Rhonda's supervised visits had to be attended by our social worker.

"There!" I said once I'd signed in the last place.

"We're all done," Mrs. Rainey said as she gathered her papers and put them into her briefcase.

"Well, Mrs. Rainey, as much as I loved talking with you over the past months, I really hope that this is the last time we have to see each other, given the circumstances."

"Now, I'll be back to do a checkup visit in a month, but after that this is one of the situations where it's best that we don't see each other again," Mrs. Rainey agreed with a laugh. "Take care, Mr. Wilson."

Once the social worker was gone, I began asking Dejah about her experience with her foster parents. I was a long way from my old lifestyle, but any nigga could die that had harmed a hair on my child's head. "Did they treat you nice?"

"Yes, they were really nice." Her smile was bright, almost radiant, when she talked about how her foster parents treated her. That was a great sign.

"Did they touch you in any of your private places?"

"Dad! No!" she said looking at me as if I were insane. "I said they were nice."

"Okay, just checking," I said, swooping her up in my arms again. Monika snapped a few pictures of us as we played around in the living room. "What do you want to do this evening?" I asked.

"I want to go to the skating rink."

"Well, the skating rink it is!"

I looked at Monika and she shook her head. "I hope you're a good skater," she said, laughing.

"It's been a long time, but we 'bout to find out if I still have it." I looked at Dejah who was sitting in front of the television, happy. "Will you take Dejah back and show her room, while I call her mother?"

"Sure," Monika said, turning to Dejah. "Do you want to see your room, sweetie?"

"Yeah!" Dejah hopped to her feet and took off running to the back.

I dialed Rhonda's number once Dejah and Monika were out of the room. "What do you want, Titus?" she answered on the third ring.

"I want to tell your stupid ass that Dejah is home."

"No, she's not because her home is here and she's not here with me."

"Her home will never be with you again, if I have anything to do with it. I'm sure you heard from the social worker that she got released to me today and that you are not to contact her unless you have a supervised visit.

"Titus, you can't take my daughter from me."

"I can, and I have. I've already came by and picked up the rest of her clothes and bedroom furniture. I got my clothes too, if you haven't noticed."

"Ooow-weee! Titus you make me so sick," she said sounding hurt.

"It's not like you give a shit, for real. I bet you didn't even notice that her things were gone out of the room."

"I…I…"

"Have a good life, Rhonda. Dejah will be fine, and probably better without you in hers."

"Titus, I'm going to try to do better," Rhonda said as her voice shook. It was kind of surprising to hear her humble down. "Will you please tell her that I love her?"

"I will do that, but like I said, for the time being, don't try to contact her or see her, or I will report you to DHR."

There was a click on the phone and then I heard the dial tone. Rhonda had hung up on me, which was fine, as long as she stayed the fuck away from Dejah with her madness.

CHAPTER TEN

RHONDA

After hanging up with Titus, I cried like a baby. While I admired the love Titus had for Dejah, I was saddened by the fact that I didn't have the mental wherewithal to fight for her like he had. If someone had fought for me when I was younger, like Titus had for Dejah, maybe I would know how to fight for what mattered.

I laid around and sulked most of the day, until I finally had the energy to talk to someone. I called Jameson at midnight. He was the only positive source of energy in my life that I had.

"Hello," he answered groggily.

"Jameson."

"Rhonda, what are you doing calling me so late?"

"You said that I could call you any time after hours."

"I meant to discuss your case. What could you have to discuss at this hour?"

"Well, this is not about my case. I just needed someone to talk to."

"Hold on." I heard him moving around, probably adjusting himself in the bed or trying to wake up. "Okay, I'm back. Sorry if I sounded rude. Usually when someone calls me at midnight, it's an emergency."

"No, I just really needed someone to talk to, and, believe it or not, you're the most positive person in my life right now."

"Well, I'm flattered," he said sarcastically.

I laughed. "You don't have to sound so enthused. I know you didn't want to wake up, but I need you."

"Rhonda, you're doing a lot of talking without telling me what's going on. Talk to me. What has you worried tonight?"

I wasn't ready to tell him about Dejah, so I sat with my knees pulled to my chest and just talked to him about my childhood life. "You know when I was a child and I used to be mean to you."

"Yeah," he said drawn out as if he had traveled back in time with me.

"I only did mean things to kids at school, because I had such a horrible life at home. My father was a crack head and was never in my life and my mother kicked me out onto the streets as a teenager after her husband tried to molest me."

"That's terrible, Rhonda."

"I know and the reason I picked on you was because I knew your parents cared for you. You brought your own lunch each day that was packed with care. You wore nice, clean clothes and your father always attended parent's day for lunch. Then, he picked you up from school each day and gave you a kiss on the cheek."

"Wow, you noticed all of that?" he asked sounding shocked.

"I didn't just observe it from you. I noticed how everyone in our class was treated. I always compared other people's lives to my own."

"That's not good. Of course, if it wasn't for my father, I would not be the man I am today. I would not be a lawyer. He taught me to be a man," Jameson said, "...but I've witnessed some very resilient people come out of much worse situations than what you described."

"I just always wished I had a strong man in my life. My father, the first man who was supposed to love me, was a very shitty person."

"I have a question for you."

"Shoot."

"Once you moved in with Shayla, didn't you get love from Shayla and her family? The reason I ask is because sometimes the people that treat us right will not carry our DNA."

I knew he was eluding to the fact that I had married Shayla's first husband after having a child by him and that I was in a legal jam by her second husband about having a child by him.

"Things just didn't turn out that way," I said, half answering the question. I looked over at my baby's bassinette on the opposite side of the room.

"But you two used to be inseparable?"

"We grew apart."

"Okay, well, can I tell you something?"

"I'm sure that you will anyway," I said, nonchalantly.

"Well, when we were in school, I dreamed that I would help take away whatever pain away that made you so mean."

"Really?"

"Yeah, it was like you were the type of girl that walked around fine and sexy, but it was something ugly about your attitude. It appeared that you were covering up the real you."

I felt so bad in that moment. I had been horrible to Jameson and countless other people. "I'm so sorry, Jameson. I was a teenager then, and..."

He cut me off expectantly. "Yeah, we were teenagers, but how different are you now, Rhonda?" I paused, giving what he said some thought. "Let me explain why I asked you that question. What I found is that by and in large, I am the same person in my heart that I was as a teenager. Sure, I don't have the glasses and small frame, and my ideas are more advanced. But all I have done is put on contacts, worked out, ate the right foods and put some credentials behind my name. My heart is still the same. I still treat people fair. I still am kind and gentle. I still love hard."

"This is true. You are a very good person, Jameson."

"Thanks, but how do you feel that you've changed? A lot of times people carry around the same hatred and pain. That same spirit that we had when we were teenagers can lie dormant, if we don't address it head on."

"I have changed," I said, hoping my words would hold some ring of the truth.

Deep down, I knew I was the same as that young girl back in elementary school, determined to spread the hurt I felt from the ones I loved and looking for acceptance in all the wrong places. I really was that same miserable person. No amount of makeup or sexy dresses could change that.

"Rhonda, taking a look at the situation you're in now, can you really say that you changed? Before you answer that, I want you to think about this question. Would a woman who loves herself and the people around them do what you have done?"

There I sat in bed with my best friend's husband's child a few feet away as I spoke. "Jameson, I…"

I paused, unable to address the heaviness on my heart. Jameson and I sat in silence for a while before he spoke. "We don't have to talk about it now, but at some point, you are going to have to ask yourself some serious questions and I really want to hear the answers, because I want to help you."

"Thanks Jameson. I don't deserve your help," I said.

"You don't owe me a thanks and though you may not feel it, you deserve God's grace."

"Jameson?"

"Yeah."

"Can we go out one day this week?"

"I would love to, but I have work up to my neck. I do plan to see you at church Sunday though."

I was kind of disappointed that he couldn't take me out, but smiled at the thought of seeing him Sunday. "Okay, here's my address." I gave him my address. Sunday couldn't come quick enough.

CHAPTER ELEVEN

JAMESON

That Sunday, I was sitting in the second pew at Real Deliverance First Baptist Church having a Holy Ghost good time. If I had to give a date, I'd say I'd been saved since I was old enough to say the word Jesus. Oh, and there was something about the name Jesus. When my father taught me of His greatness, I wanted to be baptized in His blood and saved by His mercy.

When Rhonda Wilson showed up in my office wearing that red dress and those kinky red heels looking as scrumptious as a piece of mama's fried chicken, mac-n-cheese, and collard greens at Sunday dinner, I had to get her to more even stumping grounds. The church. Surely, if I hadn't brought her here today, by tonight I'd be knee deep in her sweet potato pie.

To her credit, every single wet dream, feeling of sexual frustration, love and longing for her I had over the years came rushing back when she entered my office that day. I had to recall every Bible verse I ever learned, when she hiked her red heel clad foot on my chair displaying her perfectly manicured feet and pretty brown womanly body. My flesh wanted to drop down on one knee and spell out the words marry me on her most prized possession right then and there.

Sitting next to her on the pew, I stole a few glances at her wondrous frame as my father was preaching away in the pulpit. She was one hell of a woman, indeed. But I had to keep my life in order. In order to do that, I had to keep my heads straight – both of them.

83

After all, I was dating Lissa pretty heavy and Rhonda was seeking law counsel, which pretty much made her off limits. So that was that. Period. Happy I'd finally talked myself back into my good senses, I focused my undivided attention on the sermon.

"And the Bible says, when a man findeth a wife. He findeth a good thing. Did you hear me church? The Bible says that when a man findeth a wife, he finds a good thing. Now, some of y'all don't hear me."

"We hear ya' pastor," one woman screamed out.

"Preach," Deacon Taylor said as he sprung to his feet, clapping his hands.

"You better give the word," Sister Jenkins said in a drawn out, dramatic way.

"Aright, Sister Jenkins and Deacon Taylor hear me, so let's explore the word further then," my father said, flipping over a page of his sermon. "The Bible says, when a man findeth a wife. The first word is when. That means at the right time. Not when he wants her and not when she wants to be found, but at the time that it is predestined to happen. This meeting of kindred spirits will not happen a minute before God is ready for the meeting to happen, so patient is necessary to allow God's will to be done.

The second word is man. Notice I said man, not woman. I want you all to hear men now. The responsibility of seeking out a mate to build a family unit belongs solely to the man. A woman should not even think about finding a husband. Why church? Because it is not her responsibility to do so. That's not me talking. That's scripture."

Rhonda shifted in her seat and crossed her arms. A few of the other ladies sitting on our row looked on attentively.

"The next word in that verse is findeth. Men, this part is for you. When the time is right in your life, when you have built a temple, or a home, worthy of bringing a wife to, then it is your responsibility to actively seek her. Go out and find the woman that God has made just for you and make her your wife."

One lady in the congregation yelled out, "That's right, find me!"

I chuckled at her statement, while others just said, "Amen."

"The text says clearly that if a man findeth a wife that he has found a good thing. You women can't keep running around putting on your hot skirts seeking and finding men and then expecting them to treat you like his good thing. Because the word has already ordained that in order for a man to have a good thing in a woman he has to what?"

"Find her," most of the congregation sang out.

"That's right. Now, can I get a witness?"

"Yes!" I said, and my father went on to preach for the next thirty minutes about the marriage with over fifteen hundred people in the congregation hanging on to every word. My father was a very smart, influential, and spiritually blessed man. I admired him, even to this day.

He was right. Every man should seek out his wife. I looked at Rhonda, observing how uncomfortable she was as my father spoke. Then, I thought about the way Rhonda strolled into my office the other day with that sexy red dress riding up on her voluptuous thighs indicating that she was definitely seeking me out.

The fact that she had a child by Shayla's first and second husbands and had married Shayla's first husband told me that she had a track record in seeking love in the wrong places. She hadn't told me all the details of her past, but I was a lawyer. It was my job to find out the truth. I knew her story from the beginning to the end. From what I found out, I should definitely be running in the opposite direction, but I wanted to dig a little deeper to see if I could find the Rhonda Jackson I sought out so many years ago. Underneath her tough exterior, I was sure she was hiding and just waiting to be found.

CHAPTER TWELVE

RHONDA

Jameson was all caught up in his father's message about marriage. I watched him as he clapped and said Amen. The reverend's words were resonating with me as well, especially when he talked about not allowing our past hurts to block our present blessings.

I could not help but feel exposed as I wondered if Jameson knew I sought out Titus, while he was married to my best friend. I wondered what he would think if he knew I enticed Titus into sex, while Shayla was upstairs taking a shower. Did he know I was seeking his help so that I could get away with the heist of the century, when I stole something as precious as Shayla's new husband's sperm?

I thought I had found a good thing in Titus and then a good thing in producing a child with Antonio's sperm, but as I watched Jameson in all of his manly glory I knew I hadn't found anything until I reunited with him.

The night before, I awoke from a dead sleep, covered in sweat, with my heart pounding out of my chest. I saw the faces of Shayla, Titus, Antonio, Dejah, and Antonia. They all were drenched with tears that I'd cause to fall. I felt so bad, so hurt, as I tried to pull from the dream and orient myself to the present. *It was only a dream,* I tried to tell myself, but I knew their hurt was real.

I had only come to this church to talk to Reverend Brown about my case, but the spirit wrapped around me as soon as I walked through the doors. I thought of the things I'd done in the past, all the people I'd hurt, and a deep sadness rushed over me.

When it was time for prayer call, the sun shined brightly through the window above the cross hanging above the choir pews. That ray of light drew me to the altar. The stain-painted glass windows in the church calmed me. I still found it hard to take step towards the altar, when the pastor called all souls to the altar.

"Baby steps," I told myself gently. The darkness that I had caused others traveled through my soul for a brief moment, reminding me that I had not made amends with those I hurt.

"Have you reached out and touched someone today? Have you left anyone better than you found them?" Reverend Brown asked, as the congregation herded to the altar.

I knew those words were spoken for me, as I kneeled down onto my knees and pressed my hands together and began to pray. I hung my head low. I had intentionally worn all black to blend with my mood.

Sighing, I knew there was nothing left to do but revisit my past. Otherwise, I'd have to wake up to the aching existence I called life one more day. *How did I end up here? What happened to my life?* It had spiraled downward ever since I began to feel that my mother loved her men more than she loved me.

My mother was a very high strung, petite woman that looked like she could have been a kid herself. I remember how she used to love on me and buy me things from the store, and people thought she was my big sister. I used to sleep in the bed with her, play games and dress up. One day we were walking from the store and I called her Mama.

"Don't call me Mama. Call me Rain," she said.

I didn't know what to make of what she said to me, as a six year old. All I knew was that she was the most beautiful woman alive and I was glad she was my mother, or my Rain.

Over the years, I saw many men come and go from my mother's bedroom. Some of them were nice and would pat me on the head and give me money for candy. Others were mean and would say ugly things to her or hit her. After a while, I became immune to the men, knowing that they would only be around for a short while. Then, there would be another. That was all before she met Mr. Travis and married him. No one could tell my mother that man was not the bread and butter of life, if they wanted to.

She loved him. She worshiped the ground he walked on, even though he never had my best interest at heart. There would be times that he would tell her I spilled milk on the kitchen floor and didn't get it up, just so I would get my ass whipped. A whipping followed by days of verbal abuse, until Momma couldn't think of any more creative ways to call me a dumb bitch. No matter what she said, I held my love for her deep down in my heart. I loved her until the moment he came into my room one night. Her not showing me any love was one thing, but her allowing her man not to love me broke me down.

I didn't find any solace with my real daddy either. He was a crack head, who I wouldn't know if I passed him on the street to this day. My first memory of him was when I was three or four years old. My grandmother had given me fifty cents to get some ice cream off the ice cream truck. I ran out to the truck with my cousins, happy as hell to purchase a Push-Up.

I was so excited when I ran back into the house and plopped down on the floor beside him to eat my ice cream. I smiled so big as I opened that ice cream. My eyes met his and I tilted the ice cream to him offering him the first bite. Everyone called him my daddy, so I was sure to share with him. I thought he would be happy that I was happy and we both could be happy together. At least that's how all of my uncles were. My uncles would smile when I smiled and tickle me into a stupor, just to hear me giggle. But oh no, not my dad.

"Give me that ice cream!" he said, when I held it out to him. I reluctantly handed it over to him and he bit one bite and then another, until almost three quarters of the ice cream was gone. He gulped the remaining piece down like it wasn't nothing. "Shut up!" he said, when I began to cry as he took the last bite.

I remember my three-year-old brain thinking, in that very moment, that he wasn't shit! I was only a toddler and I knew he wasn't shit and would never be shit in his life. I never liked the thought of my father after then.

When my grandmother found out what he had done, she fussed at him. She went to the store and bought me a box of Push-Ups. She was my love. She picked up wherever he was lacking.

A week later, karma caught up with my father. He was outside trying to knock down a wasp nest and the wasp fought back, stinging him all over his body. I remember sitting there with a smirk on my face and thinking he was a big dummy. It wasn't long after that when my grandmother stopped letting him come around. After he had stolen the neighbor's lawnmower and broken in another neighbor's house to feed his crack habit, she said that was her last straw.

I had two huge reasons to not be shit. However, thanks to Jameson's encouragement, I felt I had the power to change my narrative. I had the power to recreate me. Placing one hand on the altar, I leaned forward as a tear slipped from my eyes. I had felt so much pain in my life. I had felt like I had no one to turn to, at times. When the pastor began to minister to us through prayer, I knew I was in the right place. I waved my hands in the air. I didn't just hear the word, I breathed it in.

There I stood, all polished up on the outside, but broken on the inside. Rhonda Wilson, the once popular, outgoing socialite was an utter failure. A joke. A menace to society. When Titus was caking me with Versace originals, late model cars and jewelry, nothing else mattered. I was blinded by the bling. I didn't care about Shayla or her feelings. I didn't care about anyone but myself. But now, as the spirits that I'd crossed shuffled unsettled through my mind, none of the material things meant anything.

*

After church, Jameson stood around greeting people with me by his side. By some of the accusatory looks I received, I was glad that I'd chosen a more conservative black dress and black high heels. My hair fell around my shoulders in a few fluffy curls and I wore a black church hat with a veil.

"Hello Jameson! Nice to see you this Sunday," I heard a familiar voice say. I was standing a few inches away from Shayla when I turned around. Jameson shook her hand and then looked at me awkwardly. "Rhonda," she said, looking at me with a very stern look.

"Hi Shayla," I said, nervously stepping closer to her. "I'm very sorry for everything I've done."

"Girl, if you take one step closer to me, I'm going to forget where I'm at and whip you into submission up in here."

"Shayla, I think you should hear her out," Jameson interjected. He placed a hand on Shayla's shoulder hoping to calm her.

"What's going on here?" Antonio said, after shaking another members hand and realizing what was going on.

"Mama, who's that?" little Tyler said, looking up at me with his big brown eyes.

"Come on, Tyler!" Shayla said, grabbing her son's hand and heading out the door with Antonio close behind, but not before he shot me another look that could kill.

"It's okay. They are good Christian people. They will forgive you, sooner or later, Rhonda," Jameson said, wrapping his arm around me to console me as I felt tears stinging the corners of my eyes.

"It is always a pleasure to see my eldest son at Real Deliverance First Baptist Church," the pastor said, walking over and patting his back. "Is everything alright, Son?" he asked softly.

"Everything is fine," Jameson said, turning to great his father.

"And you, young lady, it is always a blessing to see a new face in the house of the Lord," Reverend Brown observed me and then extended his hand for a firm shake.

"Father, this is the friend that I told you about on the phone, Rhonda Wilson."

"Hello, Rhonda. Nice to meet you," the reverend said.

"Nice to meet you too," I told him with the most genuine smile I could muster.

"Very well, follow me to my office, so we can have some privacy."

We followed Reverend Jameson down a long hall that was decorated with plaques and certificates of accomplishments he'd received over the thirty or so years that he'd been preaching. A huge dignified picture of him was at the end of the hall. We arrived at a huge mahogany door that screamed royalty from the uniquely carved wood to the golden door handle.

Entering the door, Reverend said, "Come on in and have a seat." He pointed to a short leather sofa that was in front of his desk. I'd never seen an office as extravagant as his. The reverend had good taste. I looked at Jameson before sitting down and he nodded his approval. I saw the reverend's eyes piercing straight through me as I sat down. "How are you today, Rhonda?"

"Much better now."

"That's good to hear," Reverend Brown said with a smile showing his one gold tooth. "Would you two like something to drink? I could get my secretary to bring some drinks in here," the reverend offered.

"No, I'm fine."

"I'm good too, Dad."

"So," Reverend Brown said focusing his attention to me. "My son tells me that you have some legal issues that you are seeking representation for, and he's trying to decide whether he is best suited to be your counsel."

I looked in Jameson's direction and he nodded. "My father is the best spiritual guide in this city, and I'm not just saying that because he's my father. He has gotten me out of several jams in my life. Go ahead and tell him what you told me and he will guide us both in the right direction."

My eyes shot daggers in Jameson's direction. I was uncomfortable telling Reverend Brown my version of what I'd done.

"It all started when I slept with my best friend's husband."

I said starting from the beginning. I exposed myself completely, telling Jameson and his father how I'd slept with Titus when Shayla was at home, right upstairs.

"But this type of dysfunctional behavior goes back to my childhood when my mother kicked me out onto the streets as a teenager. I lived with Shayla and her mother and watched Shayla, day after day, be unappreciative to her mother. Instead of being a good friend and trying to talk her into appreciating her mother, I became envious of the love that she received. The love that she didn't appreciate."

"In your own way, you wanted to take that away from her?" Reverend Brown asked.

"Yes," I said, dropping my head down into my hands.

"The case that you have pending where you are accused of taking Shayla's husband's sperm, is that true," Jameson asked, straightforwardly.

"Say what son?" the reverend asked.

"Yes, those are the charges, Dad. Are they true, Rhonda?"

Reverend Brown looked at me. "Yeah, are these accusations true, Rhonda?"

"Yes. Those are the charges and they are true."

Jameson stood up from his chair and walked around to stand beside his father. "You went inside the sperm bank and took a man's sperm?"

"I said it was true," I said standing to my feet, as well. I was not about to let them double team me up in that office. I didn't care if we were at church.

"I just can't believe you would go that far, Rhonda."

"I knew I should not have come back here. I should have kept it to myself."

"Alright, alright. Both of you have your seats," Reverend Brown said.

Jameson came back around and sat beside me, but he leaned away from me.

"Now, telling the truth is good, Rhonda." Reverend Brown looked from me to Jameson. "Neither I, nor my son, have a heaven or hell to put you in, so we are not here to judge you or condemn you, right Son."

Jameson scrunched his mouth up as if he were still taking in my admission. "Rhonda, my father is right. I don't judge you for what you did, but I cannot sit here and act like I'm not shocked."

"Though I love my daughter that came out of this situation, what I did was wrong. I can see that now. I am not proud of what I did."

"Well, the best counsel I can offer is for you to plead guilty. Admit what you have done wrong. I don't think going into the courtroom to fight this will be in your best interest," Jameson said as he pondered the possibilities. "Maybe a heart to heart with Shayla will get a better resolution for you."

"I don't think Shayla wants to ever talk to me again," I said at the brink of tears. "Oh, but I don't want to go to jail and my daughter end up an orphan. I want to be there for Antonia."

"Well, maybe there is hope. With all of your background history, there is a chance that you can get light sentencing or even off completely with psychological incompetence, if you get tested by a psychologist who agrees."

"I'm willing to do anything that will help my case."

"Seeing a psychologist and psychiatrist will definitely help," Jameson said.

"I have made a big mess of my life."

Jameson leaned towards me and took my hand into his. He stood up and walked over to stand in front of me. He pulled me into a hug. "Hopefully, instead of the end of the rope, this will be a fresh start for you, Rhonda."

In his arms, I felt that anything was possible.

CHAPTER THIRTEEN

TITUS

"Monika, you could not be better with Dejah. She absolutely loves you," I said as I hugged Monika who had just gotten in from a long day of clinicals.

Monika smiled. "I love having you two around. When I get home from school, dinner is ready. My bills are paid and I have money in the bank. I could get used to this."

"Well, get used to it. As long as you want me here, I'm yours." It felt kind of good being a one woman's man, to a woman who loved and appreciated it. I had that with Shayla, but messed up. I was blessed to find this type of love again.

"Where is Dejah anyway?" Monika asked as she peeked around the corner into the living room.

"She's not in there. Since I've been working the seven to three shift, she has her dinner and homework done and is usually in the bed by seven. That girl loves her some sleep."

"So are you telling me that I have you all to myself for the rest of the evening?"

I licked my lips and smiled mischievously. "Something like that."

"What you got in this kitchen?" she said, sniffing in the air as she walked into the kitchen behind me.

"I cooked some smoked pork chops, asparagus, and corn. Are you hungry?"

"In more ways than one."

"Girl you better calm your hot tail down before you get pregnant up in here," I said with a devilish grin. I walked to her and wrapped her up in my embrace. "You trying to get pregnant?"

"That wouldn't be such a bad thing, would it?"

"Yes it would. I want you to finish school before you think about having kids. That was important to you when I met you, and I want you to finish that goal."

"You're right honey. It's just that with you and Dejah around I've been thinking about a little one of my own."

"Until you finish school, there will be…

"No babies! Okay, gotcha," she said, walking over to the stove.

"I got you a warm plate in the microwave. I put it in there when you called and said you were on the way."

"You are so good to me," she said, blowing me a kiss.

"I try to be. I want to be a source of good energy in your life, not some nut busting dude that comes around and get you pregnant and makes your life harder. I hope you can appreciate that."

"More than you know," she said, pouring a glass of lemonade and taking a seat at the table. I stood behind her, massaging her shoulders as she ate.

"How was class today?" I asked.

"I had my Geriatric Nursing clinical and lab today. It was kind of cool hanging out with the older people and then going back to the lab to work with the dummies. Older people are full of wisdom and in need of a lot of tender loving care."

"Well, I know how that is. We all need a little TLC from time to time. I know I could use some TLC after the day I had."

"What's up?"

"Oh, not much. Just been worrying about Rhonda's case that's coming up in a few days. You know it's very possible that my daughter's mother could be locked up for some years."

"Is that such a bad thing? It's not like she can come around her anyway."

"I guess I keep remembering Rhonda in her earlier days, before she got nutty. She and Dejah used to be close. It's been hard trying to explain to Dejah that she may not see her mother until she, herself, is a grown woman."

"I know," Monika said as worry lines showed up on her forehead. "And I know I'm not Rhonda, but I will do my best to fill any void that precious little girl feels from not having her mother around. I promise to be there for you both."

"I appreciate that," I said, leaning down to capture Monika's sexy lips for a passionate kiss. I couldn't love anyone any more than I loved her in that moment.

CHAPTER FOURTEEN

LISSA

I hadn't seen or heard from Jameson in a few days, so I decided to pop up at his office. After my huge let down from Seth, I figured it was best to be proactive when it came to checking up on anyone I was dating. I had picked up his favorite lunch and was elated when his secretary told me that he was in his office.

"Don't buzz him. I'm going to surprise him with lunch," I told her as I breezed past her desk. Just as I rounded the corner leading to his office, a beautiful woman stepped out wearing a two piece black business suit and the high laced pair of stilettoes. Her hair was straight, long and black. Everything she wore was black, except for her fire engine red lipstick.

She turned to face Jameson, who stepped outside the office behind her. The way she looked at him immediately told me that she was more than a client. However, the way he looked at her told an even deeper story.

"See you tonight," the woman said with a smile.

"I can't wait," Jameson said with the strongest desire in his eyes than I had ever seen in them.

I cleared my throat, bringing both of their attention to me. The woman tilted her head to the side as if she were trying to figure out who I was. Jameson looked at me, when he finally peeled his eyes off her.

"Oh, hey Lissa."

"Oh, hey Lissa?" I said as I walked toward him. "Who is this woman that you plan to see tonight?"

"She's one of my clients."

"That's right. I'm a client and an old friend. Jameson proposed to me when we were in the sixth grade," the woman said with a sly grin. She and Jameson both started laughing, but I didn't find anything funny.

"That's cute," I said as I looked at Jameson angrily. "So, if she's a client why are you seeing her tonight?"

"We have to go over her case, which is coming up in a few days. We have a lot to cover."

"Yeah, we have a lot to cover," the woman said with a wink as she walked away seemingly unaffected by the fact that I was questioning Jameson.

I had checked her out from head to toe. Her makeup was flawless. Her attire was not too sexy, but not to prudish either. She was definitely putting in a bid for Jameson's heart.

I strutted toward Jameson and shook him away from the trance he was in as he watched her walk away. "Nice to see you again," I said once I reached him. I parted my arms for a quick hug and he obliged.

"Come on into my office." He turned to walk inside of his office. I went in and sat down. The first thing I noticed was a bouquet of flowers sitting on his desk. I read the card, which said, 'Thanks for helping me get my life back.'

"Who got you these?"

"Rhonda," he said halfheartedly. "She was thanking me for deciding to take her case."

"Is that the same Rhonda that stole the sperm from Shayla's husband?"

"Yeah," Jameson said looking upset that I would even mention Rhonda's fuckup. "Seems like a lot has been going on with Rhonda. I mean, she's sending you flowers.

eJ8

She's seeing you tonight. She's got you giddy than a motherfucker up in here."

"Watch your language?"

I threw the bag of lunch on his desk. "Should I be watching my language, or should I be cursing you out for playing games with me?"

"Alright Lissa, I'm sorry." Jameson came around and leaned on the edge of his desk facing me. "I'm going to be real with you. I can't stand here and tell you that Rhonda and I have something going on, because technically we don't."

"What do you mean *technically*?"

"I mean, I haven't officially taken her on a date, kissed her, touched or anything, but ever since she walked into my office over a week ago I have thought about her, a lot. I feel drawn to her like a moth to a flame."

As he talked, I could see the same passion burning in his eyes as he had when he looked at Rhonda earlier. "You're in love with her," I told him bluntly. He seemed to be surprised by my revelation, but then he settled in the idea.

"Maybe," he said, walking to stand and look out his office window.

My entire mood fell.

"Congratulations," I told him as I turned to walk out of the room.

"I don't want you to think that you're not a lovely woman, because you are," he said before I walked out.

"Save the 'I think you're cool, but I'm in love with her' speech. It was nice knowing you Jameson," I said as I stormed out of his office.

*

"Why haven't you been answering your phone?" Shayla said as she entered my office around five p.m. that same day.

"I've just been busy," I said, attempting to keep my face buried behind my computer. I didn't want her to see that my eyes were red from all the crying I'd done since I left Jameson's office at lunchtime.

"You must have a new client?" Shayla asked.

"Yeah and I must have forgotten to relock my door after I went to the bathroom earlier. I've been locked in here working all day trying to get Jemtech going."

"We've both worked hard today. How about we go get some drinks at happy hour?" Shayla asked walking around to the side of my desk. I knew she was being nosey and what she suspected was confirmed when I looked up at her to say no. "Aw, you've been crying. What's wrong, honey?"

"I can't seem to keep a man, that's what."

"I thought things were going good with Jameson."

"Well, so did I, until I went to his office for lunch and saw him making googly eyes with Rhonda."

"Rhonda?"

"Your girl has made her rounds. This time, she's got her claws in Jameson and there is no chance of me getting them out."

"I saw her at church Sunday, but I had no idea that she was with him. He has always crushed on Rhonda, but I would think that he would have better sense than to fall for her, much less take her case."

"If you saw the way he was looking at her, you would understand why he would follow her anywhere she went. His nose was wide open."

"Aw, Lissa," Shayla walked over and hugged me, while I was sitting down.

"Don't feel bad for me. I've been over here all day telling myself that this is for the best. I am glad that I didn't actually sleep with him, fall madly in love and then find out that he loved someone else."

"The man that's for you will come along. I just can't believe Jameson is passing up on a good woman to deal with a psychopath like Rhonda."

"I know," I said, pressing the off button on my computer. "I guess I will take you up on those drinks."

Shayla and I left my office and went to have drinks. By the end of the night, I had laughed, cried, and talked Jameson out of my system, if only for that night.

CHAPTER FIFTEEN

JAMESON

I really liked Lissa, so I felt bad about her witnessing the way I looked at Rhonda. Lissa and I met at work. My office was in the same complex as hers and Shayla's, so we all frequently ran into each other. One evening, as I was locking up, she saw me and started small talk. After a few minutes of chatting, she said she was about to go have a few drinks and offered that I join her. I did, and our conversation flowed easily. I asked her on another date and we continued to see each other and become close friends. We never took it any further than a date and a kiss.

I never yearned for Lissa the way I did for Rhonda. I prayed for discernment, asking the Lord if what I felt for Rhonda was lust or if it was a craving passion that a man should have when he findeth a good woman.

I wanted to devour Rhonda whole when she came into my office wearing that red dress. When she walked back into my life that day, it was like she never skipped a beat in my heart. She had not sought me out, because I sought her out years before either of us was ready for love. Back in the sixth grade when I proposed to Rhonda on the playground, I loved her then.

I tried to push those feelings to the back of my heart, thinking I was being a naïve man by trying to rekindle something that started in grade school. But, every single time she was near, I felt an overwhelming pull to her.

Therefore, when she knocked on my door later that night, I gradually moved to the door. I had invited her to my house to discuss the final details of her case. A meeting in the solitude of my home was against my better judgment. The smart part of me knew that we needed to meet in a public place, on more neutral grounds. However, the more selfish part of me wanted to spend time with Rhonda in a more intimate setting.

"Hey Jameson," she said, as she walked through the door. I opened my arms to give her a hug and pressed a firm kiss against her lips.

"Good evening, you look lovely," I said, staring at her intently. "How was your day?"

"It was okay," she replied, as I watched her walk straight to my mini bar to pour a glass of red wine. It was her first time in my house and she was already making herself at home. I didn't object. I actually enjoyed watching her take charge of my domain.

"We haven't even started discussing your case yet. Don't you think it's a little early for wine?" I asked her, as I sat on the sofa and took off my tie.

"If you knew what kind of day I've had, you wouldn't be asking me that," she said walking back over to take a seat beside me.

"Well, sit down beside me and tell me all about it," I said patting the sofa beside me.

"Thanks for offering for me to come here. I needed some time to get away from everything to clear my head," she said taking the seat next to me. Her floral perfume accosted my nostrils and caused me to pull her near me.

"You're welcome," I said, smiling widely. "The pleasure really is all mine." I wrapped one arm around her waist and brought her free hand to my lips for a kiss.

"What has gotten into you this evening?" she asked.

"What do you mean?" I said coyly, raising my hands.

"I mean, you have never accepted any of my passes, but tonight you've already pulled me close, and kissed me twice."

"I'm proud of you, baby. You have made big steps in getting your life together. I can see the walls falling down from your heart. It's fascinating to watch you turn warm."

She leaned into my chest without saying a word. We both reveled in the moment of quiet intimacy. "I love you, for all that you're doing for me," she whispered, as our lips met and clung.

Her soft lips and soft body nestled close to mine caused me to groan.

"I love you, for being you, Rhonda. After all that you've been through, I want to be here for you. Will you allow me to be here for you without any games being played?"

"There are no games being played. I really love you and I appreciate everything that you have done and plan to do for me, but I do have a question."

"Go ahead, ask me anything."

"You come from a prestigious family in this community. You are a lawyer. You have always been on the straight and narrow path. Meanwhile, I come from a broken home and have wreaked havoc everywhere I've been. Why would you want a person that's as messed up as me in your life?"

I put my hand to my chest so that she could feel my heartbeat. "Do you feel that?"

"Yes, your heart is about to jump out of your chest."

"Exactly. That's what you do to me. You make my vital signs change whenever you are around. My entire being reacts to you. You're the kind of woman I want in my life."

"Even with all of my faults?"

"Listen, I'm a saved man. I'm also a very religious man. I know the word frontwards and backwards, so I know that we are all sinners. I also believe that every person is worthy of God's grace, which means you are worthy."

My eyes traveled to her breasts as I spoke. They were sitting up in her bra and about to spill out of the shirt she was wearing. I took another sip of my drink as I resisted touching her in intimate places.

"Jameson."

"Yeah."

"Kiss me again."

I sat my drink down on the table and took her face in between my hands, pulling her to me. She lifted up and leaned into me on the sofa, which pushed my head back to land on the pillows. She crawled on top of me and began to move her hips against my pelvis as she kissed me to my very soul.

"Ouh, Rhonda. You feel so good," I told her, as my hands moved about her body as if they had a mind of their own. I wanted to touch every part of her and I could not stop until my desires were met.

"How good do I feel to you, Jameson?" she asked as her body slowly meshed with mine. It wasn't long before my member grew to meet her center, as it continually crashed down against me. The more she moved, the tighter my pants grew.

"I have wanted this so long," I mumbled through a long groan.

"I want you to need me!" Rhonda said as she rubbed my chest. She began unbuttoning my shirt and quickly discarded the shirt once the buttons were undone. "I want to fulfill your every need and desire," she said, as she ripped her shirt off her body.

"Stand up," I said. She did as she was told. I got up from the sofa and stood in front of her before claiming her lips again. "I don't think I'll ever get tired of kissing you, Rhonda," I said when I broke the kiss.

She smiled, and pushed her skirt down to the ground along with her panties. Standing in front of me naked, she looked like a goddess. I knew there were several reasons that making love to Rhonda was the not the move I should be making. I was a saved man attempting to bring her soul to salvation and I was her lawyer. Yet, I was a man held captive by overwhelming feelings of lust.

I took Rhonda by her hand and led her to my bedroom. Once in the room, I took off the remainder off my clothes. I laid her down on the bed and climbed on top of her, placing butterfly kisses all over the skin I could reach. I spread her legs wide and thrust inside of her pretty cunt. My first pump felt like how I thought heaven would feel. I slammed every inch of my manhood into her as hard as I could again and again.

"I'm sorry, if I'm being rough. You just feel so good," I told her as I settled into a delightful rhythm inside her slickness.

"Don't apologize. Just give me everything you have, Jameson!" she said as her body began to rotate beneath me responding to every single thrust. Her cunt gripped my hardness with a show of experience as she yelled, "Fuck me Jameson!"

"Ugh!" I grunted hard as I bucked in and out of her hot and sweet pussy. I pulled completely out and went back inside over and over, plunging deeper into her with each stroke. I couldn't think straight as my body began to tingle all over.

She wrapped her legs around my waist and pulled me to her causing me to buck wildly inside of her. I kissed her receiving her tongue and giving her mine back. I never wanted to let her go. If I could hold her captive, in this position, for the rest of my life, I would.

A loud moan bellowed from her lips as she began to tremble beneath me. Her tightening and releasing of my manhood caused me to jerk uncontrollably inside of her. Her cum soaked my dick as I came hard inside of her canal.

"I'm coming!" I told her as I pressed her legs back as far as they would go while ramming inside of her. Within seconds, my cum filled her vaginal walls and I crashed down on top of her. I kissed her continuously, never wanting to disconnect our bodies.

"Oh, you are perfect, Jameson."

"You are perfect, Rhonda. I don't ever want to let you go."

"Me either," she said as the last remnants of my seed trickled into her.

We lay like that for a while before getting up to take a shower, where we made love over and over until the early morning hour.

CHAPTER SIXTEEN

RHONDA

I spent the next two days at Jameson's house. I was glad my mother agreed to stay at my house and watch Antonia while I was with Jameson. The first night was just a taste test compared to the ways I savored his touch as he ravished me on the following two nights.

"You know, I'm a saved man. I should not be in this position right now," Jameson said, as he lay between my thighs on the second night I spent with him. "If you stay one more night, you'll have to agree to be my wife," he said bringing my hand to his lips for a kiss.

"Jameson, I would love that. I mean, one day… I just have so many of my own self-inflicted wounds that I have to try to heal right now."

Jameson leaned over the bed to get a bag off the nightstand. He took out a small box. "Give me your hand."

I reached my hand to him. "What are you doing, Jameson?"

"Remember, a long time ago, when we were supposed to get married under the monkey bars?"

"Yeah."

"Well, I was going through some of my old stuff, and I found the ring that I was going to give you." Jameson pulled out a small gold ring and placed it on my ring finger. "I remember how much I begged my mother to buy me this. I told her it was for my sweetheart and she finally gave in."

"And you still have this after all these years…"

"I kept it and I went and got it sized today. It's not an engagement ring, but it's the step before, just to let you

112

know I do care about you and I want to give us another try."

I thought about what he was saying for a moment. On the surface, it sounded good, but I didn't know if I would ever fit into his world of religion and righteousness. I had done so many evil things and he was a preacher's son. "But Jameson, we come from two different worlds. I don't know if it would work."

"We will make it work," he said kissing me passionately. "I want to make it work with you."

"But Jameson, you have so many choices of good women. What about that Lissa woman?" I said as I pushed my way from underneath him.

"Lissa is a good woman. She is…but she's not you, and I can't help who I love."

"Are you saying you love me?"

"I'm saying I want the opportunity to love you."

I wished I could have stayed with Jameson forever, but I had to deal with my court case the following morning. Love was one of the furthest things from my mind.

"Let's just take it one day at a time," I told him, knowing the following day, I could be carted away in handcuffs.

"Fair enough," he said as he sat up on the edge of the bed beside me and wrapped an arm around my shoulders.

*

The next morning was Friday and the fun was over. Standing in the court's lobby, I felt like a woman who was walking the green mile. I felt like I'd eaten my last meal and was about to be executed for the crimes I committed. In addition to the stolen sperm, there was also a lingering question of whether I had something to do with James attacking Shayla.

God knows I didn't want the idiot to try to rape Shayla. He wasn't supposed to attack her either. Our plan was for him to seduce her and then blackmail her for money. Who was I kidding? James couldn't seduce a sedated gorilla, much less Shayla.

The incriminating text I sent the night of the attack asking, *how hard can it be to get Shayla to cheat on Antonio with you? My plan is already in motion to blackmail Antonio when I get the DNA test for his baby. Stay focused, and let's get this paper*, was my undoing. It added my name to the suspicion of conspiring to commit aggravated assault against Shayla.

In the past week, I had gone to see two shrinks at the request of Jameson. My mother had been very supportive, helping me with Antonia while I was dealing with my case and when I was spending time with Jameson. She even tagged along for the psychological assessments. She was able to verify the things I described from my childhood.

Jameson gave me a look that said with his eyes that he loved me. I returned the knowing look. He and I walked into the courtroom and took the defendants chair. My mother sat behind me.

I looked over at the plaintiff's section and saw Antonio looking straight ahead, all business. I burst into tears when Shayla looked in my direction. Her quick glance sentenced me harder than anything the judge could do with the drop of his gavel. Titus walked in and took a seat on the plaintiff's side directly behind Shayla. He too was on the other side.

Jameson squeezed my hand reassuringly as the bailiff walked into the courtroom and said, "All rise. This court is now in session. The honorable Judge Kenneth Dowdy presiding. You may all be seated."

The judge read aloud some legal language and then asked, "Mrs. Rhonda Wilson, I have documents in front of me that say you are pleading not guilty, by means of psychological incompetence. Is that correct?"

"Your Honor," Jameson stood, speaking on my behalf. "My client would like to plead not guilty, by means of psychological incompetence. That is correct, sir."

Antonio gasped and began whispering in his lawyer's ear. Shayla continued to look straight ahead, but Titus was looking at me as if I was the stupidest bitch alive. He shook his head and looked away.

Jameson continued, "I have subjected my client to extensive psychological testing and have presented the results of those studies to both the court and opposing counsel."

Jameson handed the papers to the bailiff who presented a copy to the judge. The judge looked the papers over for a long while. You could hear a pin drop as he reviewed each paper carefully.

"I want to call Rhonda Wilson to the stand," Judge Dowdy said, looking over his thick glasses at me. Jameson nodded at me and I stood and walked up to the stand.

The bailiff said, "Please state your name for the court."

"Rhonda Wilson."

"Please raise your right hand." I raised my hand and he asked, "Do you solemnly swear that the testimony you are about to give is the truth, the whole truth, and nothing but the truth?"

"Yes, I do." I sat down at the witness stand and began to twiddle my thumbs.

"Rhonda, I called you up here, because I want to make sure you understand the charges levied against you and the plea that you are entering."

"Yes sir," I said, as Judge Dowdy's accusatory glance caused an unshakable fear to creep up my spine.

"You are charged with stealing property from a sperm bank with the intent to impregnate yourself and blackmail the person whose sperm you stole for money. That in itself is extortion." He paused and looked at me. "There's also a second underlying charge that you conspired in an aggravated assault against Mrs. Shayla Davis. The court is asking me to determine if this charge has any merit. Do you understand the charges against you?"

"Yes sir. I understand that and I admit that I did steal the sperm from the sperm bank, but I did not conspire for an attack against Shayla." The entire courtroom gasped loudly and some began small chatter. I guessed they didn't expect me to admit my wrongdoing so easily.

"Order in the court!" Judge Dowdy said as he pounded his gavel twice. Once the courtroom was quiet again, he continued his questioning. "Can you explain the text messages here that you sent Mr. James LaQuinn on the night that he was killed in the Davis' home?"

"Yes, in that message I asked James what was taking him so long to seduce Shayla. He said he was going to start a relationship with Shayla, so I could get to her husband. I didn't plan for him to, nor want him to, hurt her in any way," I said looking at Shayla as several people in the courtroom gasped loudly again.

"So you are admitting that you stole the sperm, but denying the charge of conspiring to have Mrs. Davis attacked?"

"That is exactly what I'm saying, I only…" I began to say to the judge before Jameson interjected.

"Your Honor, with all due respect, this line of questioning seems out of order, given that we haven't had a chance to present our case yet."

"Mr. Brown, I am trying to determine if the plea, not guilty by reason of psychological incompetence, will be allowed. My addressing your client is allowing me the ability to assess her plea. Do not interrupt again, Counsel."

"Yes sir," Jameson said, visibly thrown off by what the judge was saying to him.

"Mrs. Wilson, did you conspire with James LaQuinn in an assault against Shayla Davis?"

"No sir, I did not. James was attracted to Shayla and I thought it would be perfect if he got with Shayla. I didn't want him to attack her. I wanted him to get close to her and once he did we were going to expose her affair to her husband. By that time, I would have seduced Antonio, be pregnant with his child and we could be together." I knew my plan sounded nonsensical as I recited it to a roomful of people.

"So, taking the sperm was all a part of an intricate plan to get yourself a love affair with Mr. Davis?" the judge asked with a raised eyebrow.

"Yes sir. It was a stupid plan, and I'm not proud of it, but that's what I did."

"Okay, Rhonda, you may go back to your seat," Judge Dowdy said with a deep breath. He returned his attention to Jameson. "Mr. Brown, you want my court to believe that Mrs. Wilson is a woman who was intelligent enough to set up a plan like the one she just described, but that she is mentally incompetent today. Now is your opportunity to please explain further."

"That is exactly the situation, sir. In fact, the evidence is in the documents presented to you. What those documents show is that there are events that happened in Rhonda Wilson's childhood that led to her dysfunctional behavior in seeking attention of men. It also shows that the brunt of her dysfunction was directed toward an obsession to have Shayla Davis' life." The judge flipped through the pages of the file as Jameson talked.

"I see in here where it says that Mrs. Wilson had an affair with Shayla's first husband and, when she found it impossible to seduce her second husband, she came up with a plan to take him away by other means," Judge Dowdy said as he read the psychiatrist's statement.

"Mrs. Wilson has a history of going from one dysfunctional extreme to another where her relationships are concerned." Jameson paused for a moment as if he were internally registering what he'd just said. When he recovered, he added, "It is my belief, as well as the belief of two highly trained professionals, both a psychologist and a psychiatrist, that the decisions Rhonda is making today are based on past events in her life."

"So are the decisions the rest of the world is making. She's not the only one that comes into my courtroom with a past. Tell me something that will give grounds to eliminate or lighten her sentencing."

"Your Honor, if I may speak." I looked to Jameson for forgiveness for interrupting.

"Sure, might as well," Judge Dowdy said, irritated.

"I am not using the fact that my father never loved me, or that I was molested by my mother's husband and kicked out the house when I was sixteen as a crutch. I am not using the fact that I wouldn't know my father if I passed him on the street or how when my mother kicked me out there were no relatives there to take me in." I looked at my mother who swallowed the lump in her throat. Tears flew from my eyes as I said, "Shayla Davis was the only person who would take me in, but there was something insanely wrong with me, because I didn't accept her love genuinely.

When I moved into Shayla's home as a teenager, instead of appreciating what she'd done for me, I began to envy her. I didn't like that she had people who loved her in her corner every step of the way, and yet I was abandoned. I thought I was owed better. Secretly, I thought I was owed what she had. However, I've come to understand my faults, thanks to Jameson and his father counseling me. This is not just a court case I'm trying to beat. I'm trying to get my life back."

"Your Honor, may I have permission to speak?" Antonio's lawyer, Brock Gordon, stood and asked.

"You may."

"Thank you," he said to the judge and then waved his hand around to recognize Jameson and myself. "This is quite a show that my colleague, Mr. Brown, and the defendant have going here, but Your Honor, you already summed this up. People who are mentally incompetent do not conspire to do the things that Rhonda Wilson did."

"But Your Honor," Jameson interjected. "You can be mentally incompetent, but…"

"Allow him to finish," Judge Dowdy said raising his hand to halt Jameson.

119

"My client and his wife received a hefty settlement from Forge Sperm Bank and that is all fine and well. What we are seeking today is justice for Rhonda's part in this whole debacle. As short as a few weeks ago, Mrs. Wilson sent a picture of her daughter to my client, taunting him with a child that he didn't consent to her making." Jameson shot me a surprised look. "She has also demanded child support, which further proves that she has sense enough to seek money like the money hungry woman that she is."

"Okay Counsel, I get your point," Judge Dowdy said.

"Thanks Your Honor," Brock said adding, "…at the very least, we want to see a ruling that says my client has no responsibility for the Rhonda's child that was a result of this sperm scandal."

"Have you looked over the documents?" Jameson asked Brock.

"Of course, I have," Brock said, arguing back and forth with Jameson about my culpability for a short while before Judge Dowdy interrupted.

"That's enough, Counsel. I'm ready to issue my ruling." The judge thumbed through a law book in front of him. "According to the Martinez versus Johnson case of 1989, where Angela Martinez took a baby from a nursery and lived with the child as if she were her own for five years because she had obsessed over Lidia Johnson's child, a plea of mental insanity can be used in a case where the defendant has extreme childhood issues that may affect the way they adapt to society."

Jameson looked at me, hopeful.

"But I don't one hundred percent agree that people like this are not menaces to society. However, I am a judge not a psychologist or a psychiatrist. Since two trained mental health professionals have agreed that you were mentally incompetent at the time the said crimes were committed, I am going to give you two options.

Option number one is to pay the plaintiff the sum of one million dollars over an eighteen year period. If you are not able to make these payments, then you will be indebted to the court and could face jail time in the future.

Option number two, you agree to be released to the Georgia State Mental Institution, where you will remain until such time as you receive the mental help that you need, before you are released on your own recognizance. No payments will be due to the plaintiff with this option."

"I don't have a million dollars!" I said, as I thought of the time I had already lost and the future time I'd loose with my precious babies. "Who will take care of my kids, if I go to a mental hospital?"

"I have Dejah in my custody," Titus spoke up matter-of-factly.

"Thank you, Titus! You are a great father."

"I will take care of Antonia, Rhonda," my mother spoke up, as well.

"Thank you," I said, tearfully appreciating my mother. As I looked at my mother, I thought about how little she did for me when I was growing up. Maybe she would be able to make up for it through Antonia.

"Order in the court!" Judge Dowdy yelled, cutting off the moment I was having with Titus and my mother. When there was order again, he spoke, "Which option do you chose, Mrs. Wilson?"

"Your Honor, I will take the second option and receive mental health treatment."

"Good. The court secretary has entered in that option as my judgment. As for the child that resulted from the stolen sperm, my ruling is that Mrs. Rhonda Wilson is one hundred percent responsible for the care of this child. She, nor anyone on her behalf, may contact Mr. or Mrs. Davis regarding caring for, spending time with, or any expenses otherwise related to one Antonia Wilson."

My heart ached as I thought about my daughter. I didn't know how long I would be gone or if she would remember me when I came back.

I looked at Jameson who had tears building in his eyes. "This battle is not lost. I will continue to fight for you. Meanwhile, I want you to get the treatment you need. I'll be there every day to see your beautiful face. I promise," he whispered. It was not long after that before I was escorted out of the courtroom and into the custody of the mental hospital.

"Shayla, I'm so sorry for everything I've ever done to you," I yelled as I passed Shayla on the way out. She didn't utter a word. She just rolled her eyes and walked out past me and of the courtroom.

I looked back at my mother and pleaded with my eyes for her to care for my daughter the way she never cared for me. I thought about Dejah and Titus, and looked in the direction where Titus had been sitting. He too was gone, but I was happy that he had custody of our beautiful daughter. She had a father who loved her and I hoped that one day I would be able to give her the genuine love she deserved, and prove worthy of her love in return.

I deserve everything coming my way and more, I thought as I walked out of the courtroom with my hands covering my eyes.

THE END

Note from the Author:

Thanks for reading Secrets of a Kept Woman 3, the final book in the Secrets series. It has been a joy working with this series. While many of the lessons in this series were pulled from my past experience, for the most part the characters have taken on a life of their own. In the end though, I felt Rhonda got exactly what she needed for healing, genuine love and psychological help. I'd like to think that once she gets out of the mental institution, having faced all of her demons head on, she will be prepared to receive the love that Jameson has waiting for her, and boy oh boy will he wait after having a taste of the woman that he's craved for so long.

Do you think Jameson has found a good thing in Rhonda?

Leave a review on Amazon with your answer ☺

EXCERPT

BREATHLESS:
In Love With An Alpha Billionaire
Now Available on Amazon!

***

CHAPTER ONE

DESTINY

What in the Hell?

What is it about Jacob Turner? I wondered, as I sat naked in the center of his circular, king-sized bed in his presidential suite at the Marriott Marquis. I'd left my office to go get a cup of coffee around noon, and hours later I was about to open myself up to a stranger who'd literally charmed my panties off.

If anyone had told me I would bump into the heir of Turner Enterprises and be in the billionaire's bed by nightfall, I would have cursed them out for suggesting something like that about me. Turner Enterprises was the nation's number one commercial construction conglomerate that had been passed down for generations through the Turner family. It had offices all over the United States. Every substantial piece of business property in the U.S. was constructed by Turner Enterprises.

I could understand why Jacob was such a persuasive

man. He had been groomed since he was old enough to walk, to take the helm of the business. He was powerful, and damned sure influential. He had influenced me to forget all my values and come back to his suite, after hours of mentally stimulating conversation.

I looked around at the lavish room and felt out of place. "Jacob, I don't think I should be here," I said, while scooting to the edge of the bed.

He pulled me back to him, hard. "Stay," he said, breathing his hot breath on my neck. "We don't have to do anything you don't want to do, but please stay."

I turned around and looked into his green eyes. He looked like he was used to getting what he wanted. I was sure he could have any woman he desired. Why was he pleading for me to stay?

"I will stay a little while longer, but then I have to go," I said, crossing my arms to cover my chest. It was Montie's weekend with the kids, so I really had nowhere to go. I just didn't want to lay up all night with a man that I barely knew.

He slid over to sit beside me on the edge of the bed. Turning my face to his, he placed a soft kiss on my lips. I reveled in the wonderful smell of his breath against mine. I wanted to straddle his lap and swallow him whole, while running my fingers over his smooth, tanned back, but I stayed in control of my actions. I let out a deep breath and looked away, breaking our intense stare.

He sensed that I was uncomfortable, so he stood up, went to the closet, and returned with a robe. "Put this on," he ordered.

His protruding erection told me what he wanted. Nevertheless, he respected my wishes enough not to press the issue. He put some distance between us and sat on the sofa on the other side of the room. He turned on the television.

"What is it about you, Destiny?" he asked as he watched me intently. His eyes were so full of need. That baffled me.

"What do you mean, what is it about me?"

He bit down on his bottom lip. "I mean, what is it about you that has me so thrown off. I've never had a woman in my hotel room, unless it was for... you know. But with you, I'm satisfied with just watching you sit there."

"You will have to tell me tell me what it is. You're the one who invited me to your room, Jacob."

"I guess I just didn't want our conversation to end at the coffee shop. I wanted to see more of you; needed to see more of you," he said as his eyes raked over my body.

I stood up, put on the robe, and sat back down on the bed. "Well, you got to see all of me. Are you happy?" I asked, tying the robe tighter.

"Yeah...Come sit beside me," he said, patting the spot beside him. It was not a request, but an order that I followed. Once I sat down, he reached over and pulled the string releasing my bare flesh, again. He ran his fingers over my neck, admiring it as if it were a perfect sculpture. He then ran his fingers through my hair and pulled my face to his.

Looking into my eyes, he crushed his lips against

mine. His other hand had a firm grip around my back. My arms flew around his neck as our tongues danced. We kissed with tension, as if we were both awaiting a release. I hadn't had sex in months, and the way he owned my lips said he hadn't felt real passion in just as long. I wanted Jacob bad and that unnerved me. I didn't like not being able to control the overwhelming feeling emerging between my thighs. I ran my hands over his body, slowly and deliberately. He pulled my hands together and placed them on my legs when I reached his stomach.

"Touch yourself," he said, moving my hands to my own lap. I obeyed, slowly moving them up to caress each of my breasts, running my hands back down my stomach and thighs. "That's enough," he said, just as I was about to stroke my hottest spot.

What in the hell am I doing? I wondered, as I looked into the most handsome face I'd ever seen. I wondered what kind of mind control this eccentric, brown-haired, green-eyed Caucasian man had over me. He replaced my hand with his and I felt his two fingers ease deep inside of me, finding my spot, and bringing my full attention back to him. I fell back on the sofa and began to wriggle, when he intensified his strokes. "Jacob… oh… that feels good."

"I want it to feel better than good," he said as he removed his fingers and dropped down onto the carpeted floor. He slid my ass to the edge of the sofa and his head disappeared between my thighs, only reappearing to say, "You are sweet, Destiny."

He tongue kissed my lower lips as I murmured my satisfaction. He pressed his tongue hard against my clit and moved it back and forth in measured strokes. He held my legs firmly in place so I could not move, as a violent orgasm poured into his mouth. I jerked uncontrollably, experiencing some type of outer-body state that had never happened to me.

He moaned as he lapped up my sweet nectar, not leaving one drop behind. He quickly stood up and removed his boxers, as the last ripples of orgasm went through my body. He was much larger than Montie, which made me think hard about whether I wanted him to continue his plundering. Before I could say a word, he pulled me into his embrace and seized my lips once again. "I want you so bad," he said, rubbing his hand against my clit.

"I want you, too," I said, taking in his magnificent physique. Strong jaw line, broad shoulders, toned abs and thighs. He looked kingly as he stood up and walked to his drawer to get a condom out of his wallet. As I watched this perfectly sculptured, almond milk colored man walk away, I looked at my darker thighs that had lines of cellulite from when I was heavier, and sat up on the sofa. I pulled the robe back around my body.

"What are you doing?" he asked as he walked back to me.

"I got cold," I said, avoiding his gaze.

As he applied his condom, he continued to study me. "Cold, huh?" he said as he walked over to the temperature gauge and turned on the heat. He came back to me, took me by the hand and walked me to the bed.

Standing in front of the bed, he kissed me so sweetly that I moaned recklessly into his throat. I couldn't resist my attraction to him. I didn't even notice him slowly removing my robe again, until he threw it across the room, as if he never wanted to see it again.

"I want to look at you while I make love to you," he said as he laid me down on the bed.

I scooted to the center of the massive bed and opened my legs wide. He crawled on top of me and pushed my legs back further with his arms.

"Oh!" I screamed when he entered me with precision, ripping my canal open without warning.

"Shit, you're tight," he said, as my pussy gave way to the pressure of his size. Within seconds, he possessed me with every slow and deliberate stroke. I quivered with every thrust, with what seemed to be a constant orgasm.

"What...are...you...doing...to...me?" I managed to ask between the jerking and quivering that had, once again, taken over my body. When he took my nipple into his mouth, I trembled, releasing the hardest orgasm ever, all over his condom clad dick and down onto the bed. He bucked relentlessly against my pussy, so hard that I contracted and released uncontrollably.

"I'm coming! Ugh!" he said, collapsing down on top of me, holding me in place. I stared at this amazing creature in awe, as he said, "Stay with me tonight."

CHAPTER TWO

DESTINY

Breathless

Earlier that day, before I fell in bed with Jacob, I walked out of Tazi's Cafe in downtown Atlanta, with a piping hot cup of coffee in my hand. Jacob approached the store walking in a measured stride, and my eyes zoned in on his soft, green gaze. But that wasn't all that had my attention. It was the gush of fresh air that came flowing along beside him that captivated me.

"Here. Let me get that for you," he said, handing me my briefcase that had, unbeknownst to me, fallen from my hand. His gesture of kindness snapped me out of the stupor I had fallen into.

"Oh, thank you. I can be so clumsy at times," I told him, scrambling to retrieve my belongings from his outstretched hand. I noticed the handsome smile that spread across his broad face, as my hand touched his. "I'm on my lunch break and I was rushing to get back. I'm so sorry," I added, embarrassed.

"No need to apologize. The pleasure is all mine," he said as his tongue slowly slid across his lips. His gaze was piercing as he ran his eyes over my body, inch by inch.

"Do you work downtown? I haven't seen you here before," I asked, making small talk.

"No, I'm just in town for a few days," he said. "I live in Florida. However, my grandmother has a retirement home here. She told me to check out Tazi's," he said, humping his shoulders. "So here I am. Is it all that? And what do you suggest?" he asked, pointing to the store.

I wanted to suggest that the sexy creature have me for lunch, but I didn't say that. My mind wandered, thinking about lying down on the counter and letting him feast upon me. My thoughts were running away until I remembered my mantra – saved and single. Ever since I divorced Montie Brown, I'd been walking the straight and narrow. I took another *deep* breath of his fresh air, silently meditating for strength.

He ran his hand through his brown hair, and with a raised eyebrow, asked "so what do you recommend?"

A throaty voice, which sounded a tad more provocative than I wanted, belted from my lips, "Oh, I guess, the three-layer chocolate mousse cake is a winner." Trying to clean up my tone with a firm clearing of my throat, I put a little more of my business tenor into my next words and asked, "So are you originally from here?"

"Nah. I'm from Miami."

"Oh, well enjoy your first visit at Tazi's. You're going to love it," I said, taking one last look at the sexy man. I stepped around him and began to walk to my car.

"So, have you tried the three-layer chocolate mousse cake before?" he asked.

I turned around with a look of interest. I pulled my treat out of the small box inside my briefcase and said, "Yes, this push pop is a smaller 'to go' version of the cake. I order mine this way, because I can't afford the calories of an entire slice."

His eyes lit up, as he looked me over once again. I was becoming self-conscious under his glare. I was about to walk away again, when he said, "Would it be too much for me to ask you to share a three-layer chocolate mousse cake with me? You look like you could use a break and I could use the company."

He watched me as my mind waxed and waned between walking to my car and staying to entertain the stranger. I was sure there was something hidden behind every word he spoke; something intriguing enough to make me say, "Sure," as I studied his chiseled, tan face.

I entered Tazi's with him and soon found out the reason he had me at hello. Our personalities meshed like yin to yin and yang to yang; we had so much in common. We just clicked and before the end of the night, I was entangled in his web as well as his covers. I remember hearing Chris Brown and Jordin Sparks sing their duet, "No Air" years ago, and thinking the lyrics were stupid. I shook my head at the thought of being unable to breathe without a man. It was laughable. Something as essential as air was nonnegotiable for me... before I met Jacob Turner.

I had a fulfilling job that I enjoyed, a beautiful home, dependable car and two charming kids to boot. I was newly divorced, and my ex-husband was pretty decent at co-parenting, too. After signing my divorce papers, I vowed to spend some time enjoying the single life with the return of my maiden name, Destiny Baker. I needed time off from the thing so many people called love. I had soul searching to do. With all things considered, I couldn't figure out why, as the days passed by, it was so hard for me to breathe when I wasn't with Jacob.